SEVEN
AGAINST
TOMORROW

STEPHEN KOTOWYCH

Toronto • New York • London • Sydney

SEVEN AGAINST TOMORROW/ Stephen Kotowych

ISBN-13: 9780993937507

e-ISBN 13: 9780993937514

Print and ebook cover design by Kit Foster Design
(www.kitfosterdesign.com)

Print and ebook interior layout and design by
Stephen Kotowych (www.kotowych.com)

'Cladistics' artwork © 2009 by Jeff Freels. Used with permission.
(www.jeffwerx.com)

'Katana in Jungle' © 2012 by Pierrick Martinez. Used with permission.

'Saturn in G Minor' artwork © 2007 by Randall Ensley. Used with permission.

'Under the Shield' artwork © 2011 by M. Wayne Miller.
(www.mwaynemiller.com)

For Amanda—

who somehow puts up not just with me,
but with the voices in my head.

CONTENTS

PREFACE

We live in dystopian times.

Everywhere you look in SF and popular culture you see the post-apocalypse, as if on some unconscious level we're all just waiting until the whole edifice of civilization comes crashing down.

Deciding on a theme for any collection is always a challenge. As I was working up a description of the book for my cover designer, I began thinking that while the stories I write are never in a single style or genre—you'll find herein stories ranging from hard sci-fi, to near-future sci-fi set on Earth, to alternate history, and fantasies set in our own world—there are certain themes that I keep coming back to.

Discovery. Idealism. Striving to do right. Hope for the future, even in the face of adversity or continued struggle in the here-and-now of the story.

That's when the collection's title occurred to me: *Seven Against Tomorrow*. Because if our collective vision of tomorrow is a bleak one, if we seem to be eagerly anticipating massive tragedy as the only hope of achieving a better, more just world, well, in whatever small way the seven stories in this collection (and its author) stand against that despair and nihilism.

After all, the point of science fiction is not to predict the future but to *prevent* it.

Stephen Kotowych
Toronto, April 2015

ACKNOWLEDGEMENTS

My sincere thanks, first, to the editors who originally published these stories: Andy Cox; Julie Czerneda; Cory Doctorow; Michael K. Eidson; Jana Paniccia; Holly Phillips; Edmund R. Schubert; KD Wentworth; and the judges of the Writers of the Future contest. My thanks as well to Mark Leslie, who originally bought "Saturn in G Minor" but who didn't get a chance to originally publish it (long story). I'm grateful he still thought enough of it to reprint it later in *Tesseracts 16*.

Second, my thanks to all those who read and offered comments on early drafts of these stories, especially Karen Danylak, Joshua Gibson, Trent Hergenrader, Dana Hopkins, Andre Lalonde, Michael McPherson, the members of The Fledglings, and the members of The Stop-Watch Gang. These stories are all the better for your input.

And finally, I've had some great mentors in my career thus far: Kevin J. Anderson, Tim Powers, and Robert J. Sawyer. I am deeply indebted, and grateful, to each of them for their advice and friendship.

Borrowed Time

Author's Note

This story sprang from a discussion with Karen Danylak, a member of my first writers group, the Fledglings. We were chatting before one of our meetings got started and somehow the phrase "borrowed time" came up. One of us—I can't recall which—said in great SF fashion: "What if you *could* borrow time?"

Our plan was to write the story together, and when I received an anthology invitation not long after for a DAW Books anthology dealing with secret societies I knew that the "borrowed time" idea would be a fit. But Karen was busy planning a wedding and buying a house, and said that if I wanted to write the story myself I should go ahead.

This was my first fiction sale and I've toyed with the idea (encouraged by my wife, especially) of turning it into a series of novels detailing Kayla and Vincent's fate after the events of this story. Read the story: what do you think? Drop me an email to let me know at stephen@kotowych.com

- S.

BORROWED TIME

The look on Vincent's face confirmed for Kayla that she was the last person he expected to see when he answered the door. She pushed past him into the apartment.

"Hey!" Vincent said sharply.

The apartment was much the way she remembered it: looking (and smelling) of bachelor. In the half-light through the closed drapes—the ones she had made him the year before—she saw magazines and newspapers scattered on the couch, a pizza box under the coffee table, and dirty plates full of desiccated pizza crusts, and worse, sitting on top. She was sure the kitchen sink would be full of unwashed dishes.

"Still don't clean?" she said, stepping over a fallen t-shirt. Reaching into her shoulder bag, Kayla pulled out a gold pocket watch, and popped open the cover. She studied the four small dials of its chronograph face by the dim light. Each of the tiny hands turned at a different speed, some forward and some back.

Vincent gave a frustrated sigh. "I haven't spent a lot of time here lately."

"So I hear."

Vincent straightened. "What does that mean?"

Kayla's brow furrowed. The readings from the chronograph dials synched with the time reading from the large hands. She held the watch out for Vincent to see. "There's no variation from baseline here."

"Why would there be? I'm hardly having a good time." Almost at once Vincent's eyebrows arched. "Oh, *that's* what this is about. You're checking up on me. You just can't get over—"

"What the hell is the matter with you?" she interrupted. "I thought you were going to stop stealing time."

"You wanted me to stop. There's a difference."

"Because I knew you'd get caught!"

"No, Kay, you were worried *you'd* get caught. That's different, too."

"So who is she?" Kayla demanded, crossing her arms. "Another new recruit?"

"I'm through dating younger women," Vincent said, wandering into the kitchen.

Kayla's eyes narrowed. Though he'd meant to hurt her, she was angry with herself for taking the bait. The Chronographer's Guild had recruited her right after grad school and assigned Vincent—only *four* years older—to train her. He'd hardly robbed the cradle.

Besides, she'd been just as interested in him and had sent all the right signals. She'd been surprised it

4

took him so long to clue in. Light spilled into the dim apartment from the refrigerator. *Pop-snap*. Vincent stood in the open door of the fridge, bathed in light, drinking a soda. His wasting energy still bothered her.

"Did I ever get my key back from you?" he asked casually, in between gulps.

Kayla gave no answer.

"Kay?" he said. "Where's my key?"

She made no motion, no response.

Vincent's eyes went wide. "Oh God," he said. "You turned me in." He tossed the empty can to the counter. Stepping past her, he turned the deadbolt and slid the door chain across.

"I didn't turn you in," she said, defensive. "They came to me. You stopped meeting your quota, and then you stopped checking in altogether. They notice that kind of thing. They want me to bring you in."

"You? Why you?"

Kayla hesitated. "Because of our...history."

Vincent scoffed. "Is that what they told you? Doesn't matter. I don't work for them anymore." He looked out the door's peephole.

"They don't see it that way." Kayla didn't believe him, either. Vincent still wore the bracelet that, along with the chronograph, was the mark of their secret profession. A braid of rope in gold—a reminder of their first lesson, to think of time as a piece of rope, and of each moment a fiber twisting together to make up the whole. The bracelet was a constant reminder to all chronographers of their mission and oath to gather lost time, moments people skipped over, which would otherwise slip away into nothingness.

Kayla, like most chronographers, came up with her own simile for time after considering the lesson of the rope. She preferred to think of time like oil; as non-renewable a resource, and just as slippery to deal with.

"Things are so black and white for you, Kay. I wish it were that simple."

"You steal lost time and use it for yourself. Seems black and white to me. Chronographers are supposed to collect lost time and use it for the future! Without the Guild and the chronographers, who knows how much time we'd have left?"

He laughed. "Still such idealism? I always loved that about you. But it drove me crazy, too."

"I am idealistic," Kayla said. "And I'm not ashamed. The work we do," she caught herself, "the work *I* do is important, noble."

"Noble? You're the one who's stealing time, not me—you and the other chronographers."

"That's ridiculous. What we do, we do for the good of everyone, the whole human race. You know our days are numbered if we do nothing about it."

"How many tomorrows do we have, hmm?" He crossed the apartment.

"Have we ever been able to tell how much time remains unused, in reserve? The Guild would have you believe that all we have left is what the chronographers have saved and put back into use. What's that make our lead-time? A year? A bit more? Are we that close to oblivion?"

Vincent pulled one edge of the drapes back a bit, letting in a sliver of the day, and looked out across the skyscraper skyline. "All those people out there using up time, skipping over baseline like rocks over a pond, unaware of the moments they have. Humanity entered the twentieth century with one billion people; it exited with more than six. That number will only rise. There aren't enough of us," he waved his hand back and forth between them, "to keep up the quantities of time people are using. There never could be. It's diminishing returns. We're fighting a war of attrition, one that entropy is destined to win."

"We delay the end of time as long as we can. That's all the Guild could ever do," Kayla said.

He rounded on her. "What if the Guild is wrong? We could have a hundred years left, or a thousand, or maybe aeons more. Then what would that make the chronographers, if not thieves?" He crossed back to the door and looked out the peephole again. "It's one thing to *lose* time, and another to have it *taken* from you. How many hours have you stolen, Kay? How many days or years of someone's life have you taken?"

Kayla's mouth worked, but no words came out. She'd never heard anyone speak about the Guild or the chronographers that way. She was not like Vincent! She gathered time the way all good chronographers did—when it wouldn't be missed. And she returned it to the Guild, for the benefit of all to use, not for herself.

She would gather moments from the sleeping, from the excited, from the distracted. So someone would wake up feeling like they'd only just closed their eyes, or someone would see that time flies when you're having fun. Their sacrifice meant those moments would be recycled, available for someone else to use, cheating entropy of its victory for another few seconds. Vincent made it sound like she killed people.

"We all steal time," Vincent said. "I just use it differently than you."

He pulled a jacket and small duffle bag from the hall closet. He'd been preparing for an escape. He slammed the closet door.

"Where are you going?" Kayla asked. She turned as if to block his way as he headed for the window. Vincent bumped her out of his way with a shoulder.

"Vincent, where are you going?"

He pulled the drapes open, violently, ripping one from the curtain rod. It peeled away like a skin, and fading daylight streamed in. Vincent pushed the window open and threw one leg out onto the fire escape.

The sound of the bullet entering the pistol's chamber stopped him. He stood frozen for a moment, straddling the window frame, before Kayla finally spoke.

"You can't leave, Vincent. Unless it's with me, and back to the Council."

Vincent looked at her, studied the automatic she pointed at him, and turned back to the window. "If you want to stop me you'll have to fire...and shoot me in the back."

"They're in the alley, waiting for you!"

Vincent hesitated. "Nice try. But I always knew when you were lying. The Guild knows as much about bringing in a fugitive as a bunch of librarians. Don't take this the wrong way, hon, but if you're who they sent after me I don't think they bothered putting anyone in the alley."

He waited for a moment before pulling his other leg through the window. There was the sound of footfalls on the fire escape, and he was gone.

Kayla rushed to the window and leaned out. She heard him getting farther away, rattling down the escape toward the ground, but couldn't catch sight of him.

Dammit!

Strangway, the Guild agent who had assigned Kayla this task, had given her the gun but she'd never intended to use it. The threat would be enough. But no, not for Vincent. Idiot.

There was a knock at the door. Kayla checked her watch. Twenty minutes and they'd follow her up, they said. Right on time.

Muffled voices outside the door, and then the key she had given them turned in the lock. The door opened as far as the chain would allow. A body slammed against the door. The chain held, but Kayla knew it wouldn't for much longer.

What would they do, she wondered, when they found out Vincent escaped? It would be the end of her career, at best. They might let her stay on as one of the rank-and-file, patrolling every day, gathering stray bits of time day after day for years, until retirement. She didn't relish the idea of such mediocrity.

"Stop! Freeze!" she yelled. That sounded like the right kind of thing. The crashing at the door stopped momentarily. She scrambled on to the fire escape and held the gun high above her head, pressing a finger in one ear and the other ear into her arm. "Freeze!" she yelled once more for good measure, and squeezed the trigger.

She jumped at the sound but the kick was what really surprised her. There wasn't normally any call for a chronographer to use a firearm.

There were shouts in the hall, and as Kayla flew down the first set of metal stairs she heard the splintering wood of the doorframe giving way.

When her feet finally hit the ground, she ran hard down the alley. Would they know that she'd hesitated, or that Vincent had a three- or four-minute head start?

As she cleared the alley, which opened on to a busy city street, Kayla looked to the darkening sky. She couldn't take the chance that he was right about how much time was left. She had to find him. Otherwise, her charade wouldn't make much difference—she'd be finished in the Guild, and time itself would be in danger.

=

Though she had her chronograph out, Kayla relied more on feel to guide her through the city streets, in what she hoped was Vincent's direction. She found the usual fluctuations from baseline, but nothing out of the ordinary.

Sitting on a park bench, Kayla clicked shut her chronograph. She needed to gather her thoughts, focus her attention. She drew deep, slow breaths, emptying her awareness, focusing on becoming a vessel for time to pass into. Kayla waited for...*something*, some clue to where Vincent might have fled.

The glow from a hundred office towers, each a shimmering finger of glass, steel, and light, illuminated the downtown core. People in suits emptied from them, filling the streets to teeming. Each of them rushed somewhere, distracted, minds racing ahead of them. The city intruded on her awareness.

She'd never considered how many moments she could gather from these rat-race types. There was no need to check the chronograph for confirmation. She could tell there was time here, ripe for the taking; she could see it in their eyes, feel it in her bones. It would be hard to find Vincent through such a jumble.

Learning the true nature of time—that it was a real and tangible thing, as elemental as fire, as invisible as the wind—was one thing. Look at how time ravaged and wrinkled the faces of the elderly, or how the monuments man built wore and decayed as the ages passed, and it made sense. Learning the ebb and flow of moments people use but don't observe, how to take those seconds or minutes without being noticed, was something else entirely.

She had skill for it, more than some Guild recruits, and she found her own instinct often as good as data gleaned from a chronograph. So she closed her eyes, and imagined herself reaching out to them, scooping up their unwanted time like sand on a beach. Instants, seconds, moments slipped through, each one distinct to her, like sand against her skin. She could not save them all. Entropy would have its due. But she could save some.

Something indistinct pulled at her, there, over her right shoulder. Her attention shifted. There was a definite pressure, familiar...

Vincent!

Into the park she ran, deep into its darkness, with no thought of what might lurk there. He was close, she was sure, and that was what mattered.

She slowed her pace as the pressure built, like pinpricks all over her skin, like the tingle of a sleeping limb. It was right in front of her, and it was...nothing. Kayla paced near a stand of trees, feeling the pressure stronger here, weaker there, the boundaries of a bubble.

Kayla knew something of such spaces from her time with Vincent. She closed her eyes, preparing. She moved through the barrier. How seductive it was. How easy it would be to give in as she had so many times, unaware, with Vincent.

Opening her eyes, she saw the world overlaid upon itself. Night and day flexed and jostled, each trying to impose itself over the other.

Kayla was still within the same stand of trees, but there were children suddenly, half a dozen, all nine or ten years old, playing in the dying sunlight of a late August day.

Each part of Kayla's awareness fought for dominance, just as the flickering night and day did. Two moments: one theirs, one hers. Their moment was an echo for her, she realized, a flash into how they were experiencing time. Children wove around her, running after one another. Did they see her? Was she really there?

Kayla's brow tightened. Guild agents used time differently from others, were more "in-moment", in Guild parlance. They observed baseline more closely, used time at a fairly constant rate regardless of circumstances. But even they sped through moments sometimes. Everyone, even chronographers, lost stray seconds without noticing, like losing eyelashes, or shedding skin cells.

Those children, though, did not. They had every second at their disposal. There was no room for Kayla to reach in and take moments. She could feel them using and attending to every moment individually, perfectly, like no one she'd ever encountered... But how? They couldn't all be so naturally in-moment.

Until she had appeared at his door that afternoon, Kayla hadn't seen Vincent in almost a year; he'd made no effort to contact her. But now he wanted her to find him. It was the only thing that made sense.

Vincent had somehow given these children time. He knew that she would recognize the strange sensation and track it. The children were a marker, part of a trail. Vincent led her to them, and was leading her to himself. But why?

Time began to move faster around her. Kayla turned to see the sun falling behind the skyline, felt coolness against her skin as buildings' long shadows raced over her, filling the park. In the same moment, she saw the moon, the starless urban sky, the glistening office towers.

The flickering between moments intensified as they moved to merge at baseline. It was her presence, she realized, her observation of this strange sliptime, that was bringing things back into synch so rapidly.

And it was night again suddenly, Kayla's moment. The children called goodbye to one another, promised to play again the next day, as they scattered in all directions.

A young boy collided with Kayla. Perhaps he hadn't seen her, she thought, for there was surprise on his face at running into a strange woman who, for him, had not been there a moment earlier. He ran off without an apology.

Kayla began running, too, in the other direction. Vincent was close now, she was sure. And he wanted to be found.

=

She rounded a corner. Another *something* was nearby. Time rushed away from her like water through a burst dam, pulling her along in its current. He was here, on one of the restaurant patios that lined the sidewalk.

Kayla felt an unmistakable tingle and turned. Instead of Vincent, another trail marker: a blissful young couple. They were having coffee and dessert, holding hands, lost in each other's gaze.

"I've spent my whole life in this city," said Vincent, suddenly beside Kayla. "Maybe people are different somewhere else, I don't know. But here, watching people always in a hurry, always thinking about what's next, I realized that we need to do more than just make sure there's a tomorrow. We need to make sure that, once they have them, people use their *todays*. Or what point is there in keeping the wheel turning?"

"How are you doing this?" Kayla asked, awed. "*What* are you doing?"

"You're seeing what I do with the time I take. I've applied the same principles I used when we—when *I*—took time for us."

"You steal time for them?" she asked, confused. "Do they pay you for it?"

"They don't pay me." His voice had an edge at the accusation. "They don't even know what I've given them. You know they rarely see us."

Moving in moments where others were not meant rarely being seen by those people, like the children in the park, or the couple at the restaurant. Even standing so close you could reach out and touch... It was one aspect of the job Kayla knew she'd never get used to.

"I *borrow* time for them, Kay. The Guild will take other moments from them, I just borrow against that. I took a cue from something you said when we, well..."

A lot had been said the night she walked out, a great deal of it hurtful, and designed to be. She didn't look at him.

"You said I was selfish," Vincent continued. "In fact, you said stealing time, even to spend whole, perfect days with you, was the most selfish thing you'd ever heard of, as I recall your exact words.

"You know," he said in hushed tones, "some women would find that terribly romantic."

She could tell without looking that he was smiling. She smiled, too.

"That really stuck with me," he said. "It hurt. Mostly, I guess, because it was true. I *was* selfish. And one day it occurred to me: What if I gave time back? We know what happens when we take time, but what happens if we give time back to people? If we let them use the seconds or minutes we would otherwise snatch up and store away, what then?"

"You can do that?" Kayla asked.

"I have been, for months now. The results, Kay! This is what life was meant to be like! This is how it was in the beginning, how all our hominid ancestors experienced existence before we became self-aware. A perfect *now*. We lead such short, fragile lives..."

Was that a tear Kayla saw in his eye?

"Don't we deserve a chance to slow things down, to expand our finite lives sometimes? And when they have those moments people just let time wash over them, know how to handle it, the same way newborns will hold their breath under water—instinctive!"

"You knew I'd find you. You left a trail. Why?"

"Because I wanted you to see this. You are the only one who could find me. You don't really think they sent you after me because we used to date, do you?"

A denial died in Kayla's mouth.

Vincent shook his head. "Oh, Kay. So naive. They sent you because you were there when I started stealing time. You know it's possible. You know what it feels like, how to sense it. The Council knows I can borrow time, but could they track it like you can?

"It's a test of allegiance," Vincent said, turning to face her. "The Council wants to know whose side you're on. They're wondering will you turn me in, or are we in league?"

Kayla considered the idea. Did the Council question her loyalty? Perhaps they were right to. Turning Vincent in had been clear-cut when she thought he was robbing time for his own use, but now she wasn't sure. What would they do to him if she handed him over? What would they do to her if she did not?

"How are you doing this, Vince?"

"I'll tell you, but there's something I need to show you. Then see if you still want to bring me in."

He took her hand and they ran into the night. And as they ran, he explained.

=

The last time Kayla had been in a hospital was also at Vincent's side, during her training.

A tour of the coma patients was a required part of training. Whole days, months, even years could be taken from them. There were chronographers who specialized in coma patients, slipping unseen into the rooms of patients over and over... It was an easy way to make quota, but it struck Kayla as ghoulish, like preying on the helpless.

The cold and the antiseptic smell brought it back to her as she and Vincent again walked hospital halls.

Vincent found the room he wanted and they stood in the doorway, watching. An old man lay in bed connected to a web of wires, tubes, monitors, and machines. Racking coughs shook his withered frame; his voice was thin and raspy. A middle-aged man sat at his side, holding his hand. They talked in hushed tones, and sometimes the old man would smile meekly, or weep gently.

"James is dying," Vincent said quietly. "He won't last the night, the doctor says. That's his son, Derrick. He's come to say goodbye."

Kayla said nothing. She could feel the tingle of moments all around her, like an itch she wanted to scratch. She wouldn't let herself.

"The world won't let children stay children for long these days," Vincent said. "The kids in the park deserve one golden summer to always remember, so I've been giving them time for weeks now.

"That couple on the patio? Today was the day they fell in love. And, well, you know how relationships go."

Only hours ago, Kayla realized, she would have taken that as a veiled accusation. Now, she nodded her head and understood.

No matter what happened later in their relationship, the couple would always have that magical, intensely lived day they fell in love. That's what Vincent had given them. Just as, Kayla realized, he had tried to give her.

She didn't want him stealing time for her, but had she misjudged him? She considered him for a long moment, seeing perhaps for the first time what she loved in him.

"And them?" Kayla asked, turning her attention back to the old man and his son. "This is an awful time to be in-moment."

"But it's not, Kay! That's what you made me realize. With us, I tried to prolong all the happiness, all the easy moments. I didn't want the difficult ones. No one does."

He became very still. "My father died last year."

"Vincent..." Kayla took his hand. Vincent's father had been ill for several years, the whole time Kayla and Vincent were together. Vincent hadn't wanted them to meet until he recovered, saying his father didn't want people seeing him as an invalid. Now it was too late.

"It was a lot like this," he said, looking over the hospital room. "I sat with him, held his hand. We were close, I thought. We talked a few times a week; I'd go visit him. But then he was gone, and I realized there was so much unsaid. I could have taken time, spent weeks and weeks with him in-moment...but I didn't. It was too hard, too scary. And now...Now it's too late." He wiped away tears.

Kayla's throat burned. She squeezed his hand, and felt him squeeze back.

"That's when everything you'd said about my selfishness made sense. Even if we don't want those moments, even if they scare us, we need them. They make us see what we don't like about ourselves; they shake us up and change us.

"Look at this man, dying in his bed, and tell me that he hasn't been robbed of his most precious possession—*time*. For him it's lung cancer, but it could as easily have been some Guild agent who took just enough moments... I can't make him say the words, but I can give him time, and give him the chance. Time to say all the things he never said. Time to bring some peace to his life, and his son's, before the end." He turned to look at her. "If you want to put me away for that, well, you're welcome to it."

Kayla leaned up and kissed him, standing on tiptoes as she'd always had to. As their lips met she felt her resistance melt away, and she gave in. Every second—every one!—washed over her like a warm rain. She was there with Vincent, and with the old man and his son, in the moment, fully living each instant. It was all she remembered it being, and more. This was how life should be lived!

She broke the kiss when she realized the hushed conversation by the bedside had stopped. Kayla could feel eyes on her. The old man could see her, was looking at her! She was so used to not being seen she could find no words to answer the questioning look on the old man's face.

"Sorry," said Vincent. "We must have the wrong room." He took Kayla by the elbow. They stepped into the hall and back into baseline time.

Waiting there for them by the nurse's desk was Strangway, the tall, grandfatherly Guild agent who'd set Kayla after Vincent.

"Don't move," Strangway said. Men appeared at Strangway's side, and others blocked possible avenues of escape. They were the kind of men librarians wouldn't know to hire.

Cold slipped down Kayla's spine as Strangway settled his gaze on her. He knew, didn't he? He knew that she had let Vincent escape his apartment, that she now did not intend to turn him over to the Guild. They'd just been using time—had he been able to sense it? Is that what drew him here?

A pair of the men with Strangway moved to either side of Vincent, each roughly taking an arm.

"Hey! Easy!" Vincent said.

The gun. It was still in her bag, Kayla realized. Could she get it before they stopped her? She slumped her shoulder, trying to slide the strap down her arm.

"You're a little late to the arrest," Vincent said, as the men pushed him toward Strangway. "Kayla was about to bring me in. She's convinced me to turn myself over."

Kayla wanted to scream that was a lie, but his look as she caught Vincent's eyes held her back. *I know what I'm doing*, they said. *Don't stop me.*

"Well done, Kayla," Strangway said. "I knew I was right about you."

Kayla didn't like the implication.

"You know," Strangway said, stepping to within inches of Vincent, "what we do is like building a bridge of stone. All of humanity walks as one across the endless span of this bridge, except for us. We walk a few steps ahead on the leading edge, laying down the next course of brick, the next row of stones, so everyone else will find safe footing for their next step. What you do, though, is monstrous—stealing bricks from under the very feet of your fellow man!"

He nodded his head and the men ushered Vincent down the hall, through a set of swinging doors, and out of sight.

As she motioned to follow, Kayla felt an arm slip around her shoulder. She fought the urge to shrug it away.

"It's gratifying to know that you are on our side, Kayla," Strangway said. "This wasn't easy for you, I'm sure. You realize by now that this wasn't a simple assignment from the Guild."

Kayla considered the slipperiness of his statement, the layers of meaning: a veiled reminder of his secret knowledge of her crime; a kind of congratulations on passing the test and expiating her sin. It was how Vincent would have picked apart the statement, she realized. He was right—she had been naive.

Not anymore.

"I think any lingering doubts have been put to rest," he said, slowly guiding her down the hallway. "You made the right choice in the end, and that's what counts. There's no need to discuss your, hmm— youthful indiscretion?—ever again, as far as I'm concerned."

Kayla mumbled false words of thanks and forced her attention to stay in the moment. Trauma was one instance where it was easy to skim the seconds, awareness shutting down as you went into shock. She was determined to have every instant of the pain, to feel it all, remember it. Like Vincent said, the hard moments helped you change...

"It's clear you're a person of special talents," Strangway continued, "one who won't be content in the trenches, gathering time forever, yes? I have something of an eye for talent, and you have

21

greatness in store for you, I'm sure of it. I don't doubt eventually you'll be sitting on the Council with me. It might do you good to have a friend in high places as you make your way."

She allowed herself a moment of dark pride at the confirmation. Pieces had fallen into place after Vincent said her mission was a test. Of course Strangway was on the Guild Council: who else would be trusted with the knowledge that you could turn time to your own purpose?

Something about keeping enemies closer crossed Kayla's mind as she forced the effusive thanks for Strangway's patronage that he would expect.

He smiled softly and disappeared through the swinging doors at the end of the hall.

Kayla headed for the elevator, tears in her eyes.

=

Strangway wasn't the last person Kayla expected to see when she peered through the peephole, but she thought he would wait longer before coming to see his new protégé. It had been less than a week.

He knocked again.

She watched him, strange and distorted through the peephole, grow increasingly impatient with waiting. He checked his watch—not his chronograph, Kayla noted; that was a good sign—knocked once more, then turned and walked down the hall.

Kayla waited, ear pressed to the door, until she heard the elevator open and close again. She exhaled a deep and ragged breath. Had she been holding it the whole time? She slid the door chain across and decided to have more deadbolts installed; she'd seen how little help chains could be.

She closed the blinds on her living room windows—the ones she'd made herself when she made Vincent's—and returned to work on her chronograph.

Did Strangway suspect? Had he taken apart Vincent's chronograph, seen how its gears and counterweights, its crystals and wires had been modified?

Vincent had explained the basics of his borrowed time during their hurried trip to the hospital. The chronograph was the key. Simple modifications turned it from a meter for time into a *conduit* to dispense it.

How many others, in the long history of the Guild, had happened upon this secret? How many of those had the Council also "disappeared"?

She'd heard the rumors, of course, the urban legends chronographer trainees told each other. Cross the Guild, they said, and you'll end up in the coma wards, your body kept alive as Guild agents steal away every moment of the rest of your life... She'd never had reason to believe that, until now.

Was that where she'd find Vincent—a John Doe in some faraway coma ward?

And would she find other chronographers who'd made the same modifications Vincent had? Did they share his vision? As she soldered wires and reweighted the mechanisms in her chronograph, Kayla vowed to find out. ■

Saturn in G Minor

Author's Note

"Saturn in G Minor" was one of those stories that, thinking back on it now, leapt into my head fully formed. Oh, if only they would do that more often.

I read a short article in *New Scientist* about the Cassini probe orbiting Saturn and how the probe detected radio signals being produced as the icy chunks that constitute the rings of Saturn were bombarded by micrometeoroids. When you slow down recordings of these signals they resolve into almost perfect musical notes.

"Well, somebody has to get out there and play something!" was my first thought, the title for the story was the second, followed by what I'd learned of electroacoustic composition during a fantastic music course I'd take at university out of interest. The rest just fell into place.

This story won the grand prize in the Writers of the Future contest and was nominated for Canada's top SF prize, the Prix Aurora Award.

It's been very, very good to me.

- S.

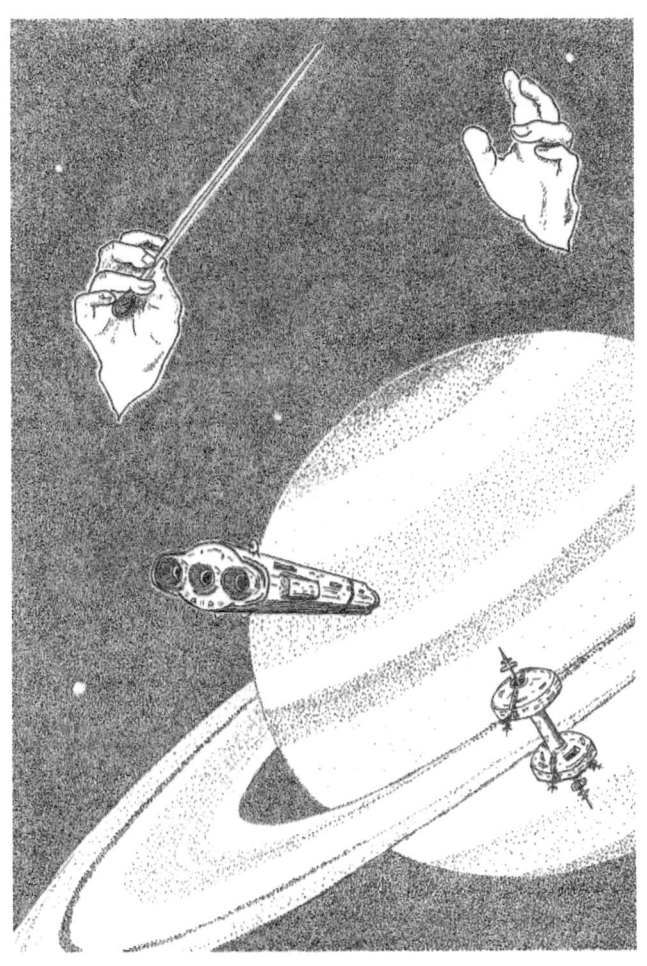

SATURN IN G MINOR

Come if you must, but you only, the e-mail read. *You must leave on the first freighter departing after your arrival. No extended stay. No exception.*

That four-year-old e-mail was the only contact Jacinto Corone had ever had with Paulo, the famed composer. Paulo lived alone on a tiny space station at Saturn's rings and, as far as Jacinto could tell, that e-mail was the only contact Paulo had with anyone, save the freighter captains, in nearly thirty years.

You must leave on the first freighter departing after your arrival.

Sixteen days. One orbit of Titan around Saturn. That's how long the supply freighter would take dropping off the new science team and resupplying the research station at Titan before starting a four-year trip back to its berth at Mars.

BANG. The deck plates rattled as a large ice meteoroid struck Jacinto's shuttle. Containers of supplies surrounding him—enough to support Paulo and his small space station for another four years—shook and shifted under their cargo mesh.

He was holding his breath, Jacinto realized, and let it escape as a slow hiss through his teeth. More impacts followed as smaller chunks buffeted the hull.

Crewmen on the freighter who'd helped him get strapped in told Jacinto to expect a bumpy ride. The shuttle's course took it close enough to the plane of Saturn's rings that hitting stray ice was to be expected. "Don't worry," a crewman had laughed as the hatch was closing. "There probably won't be a hull breach."

The containers settled as the large impacts stopped. Swishing sounds of dust and the plink-pop of micrometeoroids against the hull again filled Jacinto's ears. It was a comforting sound, like soft rain on a tin roof. How long had it been since he'd heard rain? Almost six years, he thought; the last time he'd been on Earth. He loosened his white-knuckled grip on the chair arms.

Six years of travel for sixteen days on Paulo's station. A long way to come for so short a visit. And when the cargo sled left the station to auto-rendezvous with the freighter, Jacinto had to be on it. Another four years would pass before the next freighter relieved the crew at the Titan research station and dropped off new supplies to Paulo.

No extended stays.

What would it be like to meet him? Jacinto wondered. There was so much to talk about, so much to ask him. Where to begin? He had his list of interview questions for his research—he could start there. Other questions could wait. He read the e-mail again; he'd lost count how many times he had read it before.

Everything else he knew of Paulo had been learned in the course of his doctoral research. He'd read every book, every article, seen the old documentary streams and the rare interviews Paulo had given about his rise from academic obscurity to international celebrity. And there was what his mother had told him, of course. She'd been one of Paulo's graduate students at Concordia before he hit it big.

Getting e-mail from the orbit of Saturn had impressed Jacinto, almost as much as that it was from Paulo. He'd never been off planet before, so to think of the signal coming millions of miles by laser pulse was almost too much for him to imagine. Now he'd come all that way, hadn't he? It hardly seemed real.

=

The auto-guidance computer slowed the cargo shuttle on approach to the station, matching its axial rotation. Jacinto felt the soft kiss as shuttle and station met. He waited until the air lock pressurized, and as the small light beside the door turned green he reached for the handle. Before he could grab it, the door swung open and there on the other side was Paulo.

He was no longer the suave, vigorous man from the documentary streams and old photos. Gone was the lush, jet-black hair, replaced by a thin white fringe around his otherwise bald, spotted head. A bushy salt-and-pepper beard obscured a strong jaw line. His frame, once broad and muscular, had withered. Paulo's shirt, decades out of fashion, might once have fit, but was now too big; his spindly, liver-spotted arms were lost in the billowy sleeves.

His eyes, though, remained bright. People who'd met Paulo before he left Earth, especially women, always mentioned his piercing gaze.

"You're Corone?" Paulo asked, his Montreal accent still noticeable.

"Jacinto Corone." He smiled and extended his hand. "It's a real pleasure to meet you."

Paulo took Jacinto's hand in a weak grip and gave it a few slight pumps.

"This way," Paulo said, and he inched down the corridor and around a corner. Even his steps were frail. Jacinto followed, not sure what to make of the welcome.

The corridor was white and empty except for a hatch that didn't match the station design. Paulo had retrofit the station with an escape pod. Jacinto laughed to himself. What point was there in having an escape pod installed when no one would be around to rescue you in an emergency?

Paulo showed him to quarters that were clean and prepared for a guest, but were as far from Paulo's room as could be found on such a small station. Except for areas frequented by Paulo, (which were clean and impeccably organized) most other sections of the station were run-down.

Conversation over a dinner of freeze-dried food and hydroponic vegetables was stilted at best, with Jacinto doing most of the talking. He was painfully aware at times how fawning he sounded, and would retreat into silence.

For his part, Paulo was quiet. He kept his eyes downcast or closed altogether. Wincing sometimes as if in pain, he would hum softly, without noticing, Jacinto thought.

It was slightly more than an hour's delay for transmissions by laser pulse, but Paulo had little knowledge of current events on Earth or Mars, and no interest in being brought up to speed. He didn't want to talk politics, pop culture, or even music.

"I don't know his work," Paulo said when asked his thoughts on the latest piece by Gibson-Fraser. Jacinto didn't think it right to tell him it was a two-woman composing team.

"Music today is just a derivative form of the work I was doing thirty years ago," he said. "It doesn't interest me or bear talking about."

Jacinto would have liked to debate the point— Paulo had single-handedly brought electroacoustic composition into vogue all those years ago but there had been a lot of innovative work done since—but he decided not to press the issue until he knew the man better. An argument wouldn't do on the first day they met.

When asked questions, Paulo would answer succinctly and then fall silent. Jacinto had expected he would welcome the opportunity to talk, the opportunity for human contact. But perhaps, he now thought, conversation was like a muscle that needed exercise to remain vital. Paulo's conversation was as withered by isolation in space as his body had been.

Paulo grimaced, as if in pain. "I'm going to bed. My head..." he rubbed at his temple. "You have questions for me, an interview for your research? Give them to me tomorrow; I'll look them over. We'll talk in a few days. I have a schedule of work. It won't change just because you're here. I don't sleep much, and I'm up at 0400. I'll be in the main control room working tomorrow. When you're awake we'll unload the shuttle."

With that, Paulo stood and left the mess.

Jacinto spent the next hour exploring the small station. It was the original Titan research facility, *Gurnett Station*, built for a crew of sixteen, and bought by Paulo when the new station came online. Many sections of the sixty-year-old station were on low-power stand-by or sealed off. The hydroponics garden was suffering neglect. Jacinto thought its yield could dramatically increase if Paulo put in even a little effort. Like much else there, it seemed forgotten by the station's only resident.

A great deal of work had been done modifying the other sections of the station, though, with the addition of an escape pod being the least of it.

=

Jacinto yawned as he passed another case of freeze-dried food through the airlock. He'd thought it best to impress Paulo and get a 0400 start, too. Three hours slugging cases of supplies had him questioning his decision.

Paulo, conversely, was a morning person. He was no more talkative than the night before, but he had energy to burn.

Despite Jacinto's efforts at small talk Paulo kept silent, save the occasional instruction on which case he wanted next. Even questions about Paulo's career and compositions went tersely answered.

The tedium was numbing.

Most of the composers Jacinto had interviewed for his dissertation had been only too happy to talk about themselves. Paulo's laconic nature didn't bode well for his usefulness as an interviewee, all the worse given Paulo and his compositions were the focus of Jacinto's research.

Jacinto bent down to lift one of the cases and let out a grunt when he couldn't get it more than a few centimeters off the shuttle floor before dropping it.

He stood and stretched his back. "What's in this one—rocks?"

From the far side of the airlock Paulo peered over at the case. "Yes, actually."

Jacinto turned, incredulous. "What do you need rocks for?"

Paulo smiled for the first time since Jacinto arrived. "Come. I'll show you."

=

"I call the system the plectrum!" said Paulo as he and Jacinto dumped the last of five containers of pebbles into the hopper.

"I've spent almost my whole fortune to build the plectrum and keep this station running," said Paulo. "These pebbles are regolith from asteroid mining."

That made sense, Jacinto thought. His hands were coal-black from the dust and felt like they were coated in toner.

"They're such small sizes—only a centimeter to ten centimeters across—there's not much use for them industrially, so I get them cheap from the mining companies. This is the last batch; the system's ready for the performance. The key is the size of the objects striking the rings."

Jacinto didn't understand, but this at least was a sign of life from the man. He didn't interrupt.

"I hear music, you see," said Paulo as he closed the hopper, snapped tight its pressure fitting, and mag-sealed the housing. "Air-tight now," he said, smiling. He strode down the corridor toward the control room and Jacinto followed.

"All my life I've heard music, constantly, the way Beethoven did. In some ways, I've felt a fraud as a composer. I transcribe what I hear in my head. Where does it come from?" He shrugged and keyed in the door code. The control room doors hissed open.

"I would compose, arrange, but I could never get the music to sound as it does in my head. Oh, it would be the right notes but the *sound* of them was wrong, the essence. That's what drew me to electroacoustics," Paulo said, climbing into the console chair.

"It was a very old style of composition when you came to it," said Jacinto. There'd always been a small, dedicated core of electroacoustic composers since the genre's birth in the mid-twentieth century. Once, it was even considered avant-garde—art music for a post-modern age. But it fell out of fashion, the post-modern was surpassed, and it was kept alive in university music departments. Concordia University, where Paulo had taught and where Jacinto was doing his doctorate, had one of the world's oldest programs, dating back almost one hundred and fifty years to the 1980s.

"You didn't feel it might limit you?"

"Hmmm...It did at first," said Paulo. "For years I worked in the genre. My inspiration was one of the earliest examples in the genre—the prepared piano. I turned the exotic into instruments to get sounds I needed. Remember the concerto using the Golden Gate Bridge?"

Jacinto nodded. Paulo had used the girders and tension wires as his instrument, the sound resonating across San Francisco Bay. The city still had it performed every summer.

"That was just one example. My works were always well received but they weren't what I was after."

Jacinto grinned. Now he was getting somewhere! To think of Paulo describing his works as "well received." Paulo had arrived at one of those rare moments when artist and audience are in perfect confluence, when his work had redefined the basis of modern popular music for decades. Besides spawning legions of imitators, his music had made him one of the richest men on Earth, and the richest on Mars once he'd moved there. But his compositions hadn't been what he wanted? That would be news to everyone. Jacinto wished he had his recorder with him.

"Then I happened upon the records of the Cassini probe from the early twenty-first century. Completely by accident, you understand. And that's when everything changed."

Paulo stood up and walked to the back of the room where five large objects lay under heavy plastic sheets. He pulled them off to reveal banks of keyboards, twenty in all, set in tiers along the wall.

"What the Cassini probe discovered was that as a meteoroid strikes the icy chunks making up Saturn's rings, it generates a pulse of energy and emits radio waves. Reduce the frequency by a factor of five and you bring those radio waves into the range of human hearing—tones. We have our instrument! But it's limited in range, random in its execution.

"So, we take charge of the meteoroids," said Paulo. He moved back to the console chair and turned on the computer's 3D display. "We use pebbles of different sizes, fire them at different speeds, they strike with more or less energy, generating different radio frequencies and suddenly the rings become *strings!* Pluck and strike them as you would the harpsichord, the piano, or the harp. The rings bow to our command, and the music we play—the music of the spheres!—is what we compose. All we need is an interface of some kind, a controller like these keyboards. We program them to regulate the cues for the firing sequence and all of Saturn becomes our hammered dulcimer."

"You're going to play music on Saturn's rings?"

"Yes," said Paulo. "An entire symphony. And you will help me finish it."

=

"Why won't you let me work on the last movement?" Jacinto asked over a dinner of re-hydrated chicken. He and Paulo had been working furiously for days inputting the final sequencing for the *Saturn Symphony*, as he'd begun to call it. Paulo would input the notes using the keyboards—each key set to trigger the release of certain sized pellets from the sorted hopper bins of the plectrum—and Jacinto would add in, by hand, dynamics where Paulo had indicated. The composer had it all planned out and just need Jacinto to do the tedious grunt work, as it turned out.

Rinforzando, fortissimo, diminuendo, mezzo piano—all entered as long, increasing strings of digits into the command protocols for the firing sequence. But

Jacinto had four days left on the station and had yet to see the sequencing for the finale.

"That section is mine," Paulo said before taking another bite. Back to his prickly self, Jacinto noted. That was the pattern—tolerable in the mornings, difficult at night, once the headaches set in.

"If I could just get a look at it, for my research—"

"The final movement is off limits to you, and your research, until it's finished," Paulo said, pointing his plastic fork at Jacinto with every emphasis. "It will all be done in a few days; I'll answer questions for your research, and then I will perform the symphony at last..." Paulo had a longing look in his eye, one of anticipated relief.

"Will you be returning on the freighter?" Jacinto sounded more hopeful than he'd intended.

"Why did you come here?" Paulo asked, wincing as if something pained him, and rubbed at his eyes.

"I came to meet you. For my research," Jacinto said.

"You're a young man. You've wasted a lot of time coming all this way, only to have to go back. Don't waste your time traveling. No one finds what they seek in traveling."

"But I've found you."

"All you've found of me is a cross-section, a fragment. You'll take what you want to, never knowing the whole. You've wasted all this time, and you'll have nothing to show for it."

"Did you waste your time? What have you got to show for all these years out here?" It was angrier than Jacinto meant it to sound, but not angrier than he felt.

"Ah, but you see I belong here—you don't. I've arrived where I'm going."

"You know, my mother's told me a lot about you," Jacinto said with an edge to his voice that surprised even him.

Paulo looked up. "Your mother?"

"Cassandra Corone. She was one of your grad students at Concordia."

"I know who she is," Paulo snapped. "Why do you think I agreed to your visit? What did she tell you about me?"

"Stories about being your student, seeing you in concert, watching you become famous."

Paulo considered this a moment. "You look a lot like her."

"That's what everyone says." Jacinto gave a cold smile. "She says I have my father's eyes, though."

Paulo chewed his last bit of chicken without looking up from the table. When he was finished, he stood and left without cleaning up his mess from the table.

=

Paulo spent the day after their fight in his room. It must have been a terrible migraine, Jacinto decided. He could hear Paulo whimpering and crying through the door when he went to check on him that morning. Did the music cause his headaches? he wondered.

Settling into the console chair, Jacinto turned on the computer's 3D display. He began tabbing through the program files for the firing sequence, looking for anything that might be the final movement.

Paulo seemed determined to thwart his research. With only three days left before he had to depart, Jacinto had yet to see any results from the final section, and had no interview with the focus of his research...

Empty handed—isn't that what Paulo had said? He'd be damned if he was going to let Paulo be right.

There! That menu was what he was looking for. It was the only one listing a final movement. 'Dénouement', Paulo named it.

He reached out and pushed the floating command icon to begin playback. Leaning back in the chair, Jacinto folded his arms, immensely satisfied. He'd pulled one over on the old man.

As soon as the playback engaged, he could hear and feel the change in the station. It was a power down, station wide.

Sudden queasiness filled Jacinto's stomach as the station section he was in slowed its spinning. He wished he could blame his nausea on gravity loss.

The whole of the small space station shuddered as the spinning sections ground to a halt. Jacinto remembered what Paulo had said to him about the power drain when the sequence was performed. Gravity was a luxury that could be sacrificed.

Jacinto raced through menus on the holographic display, 3D command icons spinning in the air around him, trying to find some way to abort the sequence. He couldn't find a straightforward cancel command, and worried about selecting something that would do more damage.

"*Putin!*" Paulo cursed. "What have you done?" He had appeared at the compartment door, floating in zero-g. Pushing hard off the doorframe, Paulo rocketed across the room. "Out! Get out!" He shoved Jacinto from the console chair, pulled himself down and strapped in.

Paulo punched keys and scanned the read-outs. "The sequencing is cueing to start!"

"I—I didn't mean to! I was just...I wanted to finish some of the programming you asked me to do." Jacinto's denial sounded weak even to him.

"Don't lie to me! You accessed the sequencing for the final movement. I told you it was off limits to your damned research."

"Why the hell wouldn't you show me?" Jacinto banged his fist against the console. He started to drift in the zero-g and grabbed hold of the chair to stop, raging at himself.

"I never should have agreed to let you come."

"Can't you just shut it down?" Jacinto asked. He struggled to position himself in zero-g, Paulo's chair his only anchor. "Shut off the power. Will that reset the sequence?"

"And what then?" Paulo turned, a wild look in his eye. "This station is almost as old as I am. What if the power won't come back on? Then we *both* die..." Paulo turned back to the console.

Why had he said "both" that way? Jacinto's queasiness grew stronger.

"What about overriding the controls for the rotating sections?" Jacinto asked. "Won't setting them in motion again cause a power drain and cancel the firing sequence?"

"That's not the way it works!" Paulo began rubbing at his temples.

"Stop yelling at me!" Jacinto shook Paulo's chair with both hands. "I'm trying to help!"

"By trying to destroy the station?" Paulo shot back. "It's going to take all available power to operate the plectrum and keep the station's attitude constant at the same time. If those sections start rotation, not only will the plectrum's firing sequence not run properly and the whole performance fail, but the station will spin out of control and smash into the rings. Or it may simply tear the station apart first—do you wish to choose?"

A klaxon sounded and four 2D video streams popped up from the display, each showing different angles of the station's exterior.

Taken from the station's own system of micro-satellites, two videos showed the station in relief against the backdrop of Saturn. The field of view was too small to show the whole planet, but the swirling gas clouds and the vast cream-yellow face of Saturn was still breathtaking. The other video streams showed the bottom of the station, now only several hundred meters above the plane of Saturn's rings, and the hatch doors of the plectrum system opening.

Another klaxon sounded and Paulo spun his chair around. There, along the back wall of the control room, the bank of keyboards powered up. Keys on the first synthesizer began to move in their pre-programmed dance, one at first, then two, then whole chords. Then another of the synthesizers, then another, until keys on all twenty writhed and moved as if commanded by an orchestra of spectral players.

From unseen speakers came the first notes of the symphony from Saturn's rings.

"*Merde*," said Paulo.

=

Though he'd helped program in the sequences for many sections of the symphony, as the music came through the speakers for the first time, Jacinto knew he hadn't expected this.

He'd played through sections on piano, trying to work out the dynamics from the notation Paulo had given him. The timing was strange, though, and Jacinto couldn't grasp the whole. He thought he had, intellectually, some idea what to expect when he heard the piece performed, but now...

Each note was a distinct tone and not the eerie, theremin-like noise of other space phenomena Jacinto had heard recorded. As clear as notes played on piano, but the *sound!* The sound was unique, unlike any sound—real, synthesized, or manipulated—that Jacinto had ever heard.

And the limitations of using the plectrum to play the rings gave unique structural qualities to the piece.

No bent notes were possible, no vibrato or glissando, no sustains longer than two or three seconds, and even with all the careful programming an element of uncertainty pervaded the piece. There was no way to know the composition and layout of the rings below or how they would react to the strikes from the plectrum.

The piece was characterized, instead, by playfulness as Paulo fooled and tricked the ear of the listener.

Careful overlapping of note voicings mimicked some of the impossible elements of technique—doubling and tripling notes gave artificial sustain, produced delay and echo effects.

As he listened, Jacinto realized the whole was made up of four different satellite streams. Radio and plasma wave detectors on each of the station's four micro-satellites detected the same frequencies at slightly different intervals based on distance from the source. The result was four threads of music, binding together to make the whole. Paulo had incorporated the slight delay and variations into the composition.

The symphony shimmered with texture and life.

Paulo had married the most innovative elements of his atonal, avant-garde composition with the forms and patterns of the classical. This would do it, Jacinto realized. This would redefine music again, the way Paulo had decades ago.

Jacinto turned to congratulate him on a masterwork but the console chair was empty. He looked behind him to see Paulo disappearing out the control room door. Where was he going?

Turning back, on the 2D Jacinto saw the streams of pellets from the plectrum falling like glittering rain from the station. But there was something else. He looked closer. The station itself was moving farther and farther from the rings. And it was picking up speed.

He pushed off the console chair and sailed to the open door. Kicking hard off the doorframe, Jacinto launched himself down the corridor. He saw Paulo round the corner at the near junction, turning down the empty white corridor.

He wouldn't...

Jacinto pumped his arms and legs as if swimming, but it didn't help and he cursed zero-g again. He had to catch Paulo.

His arms flailed for a hold, something to slow him as he approached the junction. Fingernails skipped and skittered along the plastic and metal walls of the corridor. Sailing past the open doorway, he saw Paulo punching in a code at the escape pod door.

"No!" Jacinto yelled. His fingers ached as he strained for purchase on the wall. Fingertips found a thin edge of the doorframe. It was enough. His body swung around, slamming flat against the bulkhead. He pulled himself around the doorframe as Paulo slipped through the escape pod hatch.

Jacinto kicked off one last time as the hatch door slid shut, his arms outstretched. "Don't leave me! Don't leave me here, you son of a bitch!"

He pounded on the solid metal door, screaming, but no answer came. His throat raw and with tears in his eyes, Jacinto pushed himself back down the corridor.

Jacinto rushed to the control room. He had to stop the escape pod from leaving. Instead, he found Paulo's face on the 2D.

"You bastard!" Jacinto yelled as he pulled himself into the seat. "You're not leaving me here to die." He scrolled through menus, looking for an override.

"Damn fool," Paulo said. "You're not going to die. There's no stopping the sequence once it's started, and it's almost time for the final movement. So listen to me!"

Jacinto looked at the 2D, tears in his eyes.

"Everything is working just as it should," Paulo said.

"The station is moving!" Jacinto checked the other 2Ds, and the station was moving faster than before.

"Of course it is!" Paulo barked. "It's taking all the station's power to run the plectrum and the stabilizing thrusters to keep the station's attitude constant. *Altitude* is another matter. I built it into my composition. That's why the number sets you entered kept getting bigger—longer intervals between striking notes. It's for the station's...for *your* safety. You can't be too near during the final crescendo."

"Why not?"

"On cue, this escape pod will launch into the rings and play the final movement of my symphony." Paulo moved away from the camera lens and Jacinto saw the interior of the escape pod behind him. Dozens of gray bundles lined the walls, connected by coils of yellow wire. "When this pod explodes it will set a chain reaction of collisions in motion—generating more notes than I could ever play in a lifetime of playing music. A last great sustained cacophony to conclude my masterpiece."

Jacinto's mouth worked, but no sound came out.

"This is the way I want it, Jacinto," say Paulo. "I've suffered too long with this music, with the headaches it brings me, the sleeplessness, the agony. There's no stopping it short of this." Paulo reached out toward the camera to kill the feed.

"Wait!" Jacinto yelled, and Paulo hesitated. "But maestro—you won't be able to hear the final composition if you die!"

"Ah, I've already heard it," Paulo said, wincing again. "I've heard it a thousand million times through every moment of my life. Waking or sleeping, it never left me. It's been my lover and my demon—caressing and tormenting me all this time. My other works have been pale imitations of this piece, simple warm-ups. A composer gives part of himself away every time he writes a piece. He writes himself into the music in ways he doesn't even realize—the music demands it. This piece—well, it demands more. I must die; it must live."

"No! Please, no—"

"Goodbye, Jacinto," said Paulo, reaching toward the camera. "You'll find what you need in my cabin.

Tell your mother...Tell her I'm sorry. For everything." The image died.

Jacinto felt the station rock as the pod blasted away. He screamed in impotent rage.

=

The tiny cargo shuttle seemed cavernous now; it was as empty as Jacinto felt. It was only a few hours before the rendezvous with the freighter, not that Jacinto relished the idea of company.

On a handheld, he scrolled through the answers Paulo had left to his research questions. Paulo had never intended to sit down for an interview, instead writing paragraph after paragraph of response for Jacinto to sort through later. It would make a ground breaking thesis, but the thought brought Jacinto no joy.

He'd gathered up Paulo's few possessions and fit them all in two small cargo shells for the journey home. Paulo had left a will, too, though Jacinto hadn't the heart to read it.

A recording of the symphony played over the shuttle speaker system. It was so loud the speakers crackled with distortion; the volume was almost painful. The station's computer had recorded the whole piece as it played out, so that was preserved at least. It was the first and last performance of the *Saturn Symphony*, Jacinto thought. No one could imitate Paulo this time. There would be no derivatives.

On the four-year voyage home, Jacinto knew he would listen to the *Saturn Symphony* as many countless times as he'd read that brief e-mail on the journey out. And he would cry each time, as he did now.

He had the shuttle's 2D on, the exterior camera trained behind him. The station was long since out of view. Momentum from the plectrum would carry it far into space.

Instead, Saturn filled the screen. He couldn't see the whole planet, perhaps just a quarter. But the width of its rings was clear enough. A dark bruise marked the a-ring, where Paulo had struck his final chord. Matter spilled out into the Cassini Gap and toward the b-ring like salt spilled against the blackness of space.

Saturn's rings turned slowly, like an old gramophone record, playing their endless symphony.■

Gagiid

Author's Note

This story was inspired by an article (and later book) by John Vaillant about the felling of *Kiid K'iyaas*, a golden spruce sacred to the Haida peoples of British Columbia. I've always felt a great love for trees, and the story of this particular tree moved me deeply.

Originally published in the British SF magazine *Interzone* under the title "A Time for Raven," I reprint it here under its original and more appropriate title "Gagiid," (pronounced *gah-geet*) which a friend talked me out of using, and for which I've still not forgiven him, since all the reviews said something like: "Good story—but what's the deal with the title? It has nothing to do with the story…"

A funny side note: I'd written a draft of this story before going to Australia, where I tried (and failed) surfing. As the undertow dragged me to the bottom of the Pacific I recall thinking, very calmly, "Oh, *this* is what it's like to drown." Happily, I washed up on shore and later reworked a climactic scene in which a kayak is overcome by waves. I can attest to its realism.

Write what you know, right?

- S.

GAGIID

Fog had hidden Haida Gwaii from outsiders since the Beginning, from the time of Raven, until Captain Cook arrived in the eighteenth century. It was good of the captain, thought Wilson Gwaeskun, to discover his Haida ancestors who never knew they were lost.

With a double-bladed paddle Wilson pushed his kayak from shore, into the fog and the swift current of the Yakoun River. Fog wouldn't stop him. He'd dreamt of the river of late, of paddling; dreamt of glassy river stones sliding from sight beneath dark water, and he with them.

Not dreams but visions, Wilson decided. The first Haida had washed up on shore in a cockleshell and were freed by Raven. Now, Raven called Wilson back to the waters of his ancestors, to the ocean, to be finally released.

So let the waves take his body and smash his kayak. Let him become *gagiid*—the One Carried Away, the wild spirit from ancient songs born when a kayaker was lost at sea. Let the water cleanse his spirit and bring him peace as he disappeared into the depths.

Mists wrapped the forested banks, moving upon the face of the water. In the west, great billows of low cloud obscured wooded mountain peaks, like rolling avalanches frozen in mid-slide.

The cool slick of moisture against his skin did nothing to soothe the fiery ache in Wilson's shoulders and hands as he paddled. He rested a moment, feeling the strong grip of the current pull the kayak downriver.

His hands, with their swollen knuckles and the thin, translucent skin of age, were so different, he thought, from the strong hands of his days as a timber surveyor, from the hands that had paddled the Yakoun with Madeline.

By the end of her illness she'd no longer remembered him. He'd visited her grave a final time before setting out, apologizing that after more than fifty years of marriage he wouldn't be buried by her side.

The scents of pine needles, damp loam, and water full of living things hung in the air. Underneath were hints of mouldering leaves, fish washed up on shore, the sweet of rotting wood.

Indistinct at first, a skeletal form emerged from the haze. Jutting from the forested point of a small island, a denuded spruce tree lay where it had fallen years before. Its top branches stretched out over the flowing water as if the limbs—bare but for a few dead needles—reached for help from the far shore.

Wilson felt a twinge of panic seeing the tree again. His eyes darted to the front hull compartment of his kayak, his mind filling with thoughts of his cargo and of Hank Delaney. A sliver of anxiety slipped like a knife between his ribs. He took deep breaths and tried to focus on paddling.

He remembered when the prone Sitka—already covered by thick moss in the wet and damp of Haida Gwaii—stood fifty meters tall, a golden beacon shining through the forest green. *Kiid K'iyaas* they called him, the only tree the Haida ever named—grandfather of the forest, sacred to the people.

To the scientists the Golden Spruce (as the Anglos called it) was a mutant—"chlorotic" they said. It lacked the pigments that act like sunblock in the needles of a normal tree, and should have scorched. A tree covered in yellow needles meant a tree that was already dead.

Yet *Kiid K'iyaas* lived and thrived for five hundred years, its needles luminous since before Captain Cook laid eyes on them.

Wilson wasn't surprised by the confusion. *Kiid K'iyaas* was a gift of the Creator, and neither was so easily understood.

What few but the Haida knew was that *Kiid K'iyaas* had been human once. Long ago, when the ancestors mistreated each other and the land, the Creator buried their villages under snow. An old man and a boy hid under a spruce plank and were the only ones to survive. When the Creator found them, he told them to flee up the Yakoun River without looking back, lest they remember and repeat the mistakes of the others.

But the boy disobeyed, and for his defiance was transformed into the Golden Spruce.

On the near shore a grey-brown seal, resting after chasing Chinook through snaking forest rivers, roused himself from the base of a sheltering red cedar. The seal bobbed up and down as he called, comical with his underbelly covered in pine straw and dirt.

Did the seal bellow at him, Wilson wondered, or at the bear whose slick-furred head poked from the water as it paddled silently by the far shore?

Wilson felt unworthy of such a send-off.

Haida tradition said the tree would stand until the last generation. When it was cut down, the born-again preacher in town said it was God's sign to the Haida that they lived in the End Times, and that the last of them holding to pagan ways needed to get saved and get ready for the Rapture.

Wilson, though, didn't think the Creator wanted *Kiid K'iyaas* dead any more than did the Haida.

How could someone understand a life spanning centuries? You could look at the exposed stump of the tree, where the chainsaw had chewed across, and travel time on its rings.

When the tree was born, Columbus was sailing from Spain. There was a ring for the Reformation. There was another for the English Civil War. The American Revolution and their Civil War. Confederation. Two World Wars. Man walking on the moon. There, a ring when Shakespeare was born; there, one when he died. Rings for Mozart, Newton, Lincoln, Lenin, Einstein. That's what the Anglos would see, anyway.

Wilson saw a ring when Cook visited Haida Gwaii, putting it on a map so others could follow. He saw rings marking the years of smallpox that wiped out all but a few hundred Haida. Rings for Chief Koyah, Chief Wiah, Chiefs Stiltla, Ninsingwas, Skidgate and the rest.

All brought to an end by one man working a chainsaw in the dead of a winter's night.

=

There was no getting a kayak into the water from the end of the Golden Spruce Trail, and nowhere on the far shore to land. Swimming would have been the only way across. Wilson could imagine Hank Delaney slipping into the frigid winter Yakoun, naked as a serpent, dragging his clothes and chainsaw sealed in plastic.

The near-freezing water would have killed an ordinary man, but Wilson had seen Hank take similar swims in the Yakoun at all times of year. If Wilson could believe anyone getting across the twenty-meter stretch of the fast-flowing Yakoun it was Hank Delaney.

And the tree had come down, hadn't it?

Up the far bank Delaney had slithered and, working only by whatever light he'd brought, wasted no time in butchering *Kiid K'iyaas*.

First, the thick buttress ridges that helped stabilize the hulking tree. He sliced them off the same way Wilson had seen men carve thick, meaty fins from sharks and whales. Then to the trunk, four and a half meters in diameter, where deep wedge gashes gave him access to the interior. Window-block cuts through the heartwood fatally weakened the tree. His chainsaw roaring for hours, Delaney positioned his cuts and wedges so the tree would fall toward the river when the next strong winds blew...

And then he was gone, slipping back into the chill waters, leaving *Kiid K'iyaas*, mortally wounded, teetering uncertainly in the night.

=

How long had he been paddling? Maybe hours. Maybe forever. He couldn't see the shoreline—was he even moving? In a flash Wilson imagined the whole world disappeared. All that remained was the ten or twelve meters of water all around him and the mist. He closed his eyes and breathed deep, in and out, in and out, feeling cool moisture fill his nostrils, paddling all the while.

As he opened his eyes the mass of an island ghosted from the fog. Stripped bare of trees down to weather-bleached stumps it was a white, bloated corpse adrift in the water.

The eastern face of the island had slipped and given way. Tiny green tufts clung here and there along the five-kilometre long landslide. University students had probably planted the seedlings a summer or two ago at the behest of some logging company, a few months spent in the woods saving the environment.

Wilson turned his kayak away and fog enveloped the island like a funeral shroud, hiding it from view. His guilt slunk back down inside him and hid again, too.

=

During his days as a timber surveyor Wilson had scouted virgin stands, laying out logging roads for crews that would come and clear-cut huge swaths of forest. Sometimes he wondered how many trees he'd helped cut down, how much of the old growth his ancestors had known.

In some abstract way he'd known the roads he laid brought loggers and their machines, that the trees he scouted would end up as timber or pulp and paper. But he'd always moved on to the next scouting project before it happened: a timber scout who'd never seen a clear-cut.

So there was no more startling an experience in Wilson's life than moving in a single step from the loamy darkness of dense old-growth to the barren moonscape of a clear cut so big you couldn't see the other side. The move from living trees and rich earth to cutting slash and eroding soil was as drastic as the end of a fall from a tall building.

Someone once told Wilson you could see some of the big, starfish-shaped clear-cuts from space. He didn't know if it was true, but he could believe it.

He remembered crying.

Wilson was long retired when he met Hank Delaney. Hank was a forest technician; one of the best, as Wilson understood. He specialized in the high-altitude timber too difficult and too expensive to get in Wilson's day, when trees were still growing at lower elevations.

But when Hank came back from a road-marking trip up near the Alberta border, he was a changed man. There was fervour in his voice, fire in his eyes.

That's when Wilson took notice of him. There had been no environmental movement when Wilson worked the timber, no protestors spiking trees as they had in Clayoquot Sound in the '90s. He wished later that someone had said something. He wished he'd said something. But no one did, until Hank Delaney.

Hank's commitment to protecting the forest amazed Wilson—it was a convert's zeal and it fired Wilson's soul. Usually the white man found his religion in the desert places of the world. But Hank found religion up there, amongst the trees. Maybe it found him.

For a time Grant kept his job surveying with the timber companies, but his reports soon became difficult for the companies to deal with. He started arguing for huge tracts of prime timber to be set aside and protected. When that didn't work, vitriolic attacks of the companies and their logging methods were included right in the reports. It wasn't long before he was out of a job.

=

Wilson came back to himself as the bottom of the kayak scrapped rock. He'd been lost in the rhythm of his paddle stroke, zoned out staring at the front cargo hold. The bottom shouldn't be so shallow... Where was he?

Though mists shrouded the shore, Wilson had entered the mouth of a narrow forest river. But one he didn't know about? The river flowed east, which meant it emptied into the ocean. He decided to follow its course to the Hecate Strait.

The Anglos had named the straight for the Greek goddess of witchcraft and the land of the dead. The Hecate was known for overfalls and blind roller waves ten to twenty meters high, and waves that ricocheted back and forth off cliff faces, picking up speed to form a mass of roiling, malevolent ocean.

Perhaps it wasn't such a bad name after all, Wilson thought. He would know soon enough.

When Hank finally related the vision he'd had, Wilson wasn't surprised in the least. He'd always suspected something of the sort.

Hearing Hank speak of the experience made Wilson finally understand why prophets and mystics seemed to speak in riddles. He could speak of the vision only in impressions: of being in the woods one moment and then *being* the trees the next; of his profound connection with the natural world on every level of being; of a wholeness in the experience not present in daily life. And there was the call, a sense of mission.

It was clear enough to Wilson that call had come from the Creator, and that Hank would fulfill a destiny to protect the forests.

But not everyone was so accepting of Hank's vision.

Doctors diagnosed him as paranoid schizophrenic. Hank said they worked for the logging companies that were persecuting him and ruining his reputation. He blamed the same companies for the foreclosure threats against his house, for the restraining orders.

Without a job and refusing to take his meds, it wasn't long before Hank's wife left, taking their two children. He blamed the logging companies for that, too.

Years earlier, other doctors said Wilson's friend Bill, a tribal shaman, was mentally ill. It didn't bother Wilson. Maybe you had to be schizo to be a shaman, to tune in the voices of the ancestors, of nature, of the Creator. Hank spoke the truth and Wilson knew it.

But the fury that Hank vented toward the logging companies soon turned on the Haida and other locals.

He accused them of 'collaborating' with the logging companies, and used the Golden Spruce as his example.

The island the Golden Spruce grew on was part of a timber company set-aside. Package tours hauled busloads of people to the site every year, like a forest theme park; on the far side of the ridge behind them hundreds of square kilometres were stripped bare. None of the tours ever went there.

Why was one tree so special, he asked, when countless others were not? Why keep the Golden Spruce like a pet and let so many other trees die?

It was then, Wilson later realized, that Hank had decided to make an example of *Kiid K'iyaas*.

=

The morning after he'd butchered the Golden Spruce, before anyone knew what had happened, Hank gave Wilson his chainsaw.

He'd moved into the Golden Spruce Inn, of all places, and went about giving away all his possessions. Wilson couldn't forgive himself for not realizing his friend was making preparations, saying good-byes. Did Delaney know he wasn't long for the world once he cut down *Kiid K'iyaas?*

Having no need for the chainsaw Wilson took it anyway, out of friendship. He could always give it back later. The chain was well oiled, the engine greased, the handle sticky with sap. When Wilson realized days later where the sap came from, he felt like the chainsaw was covered in blood.

Wilson had often wondered why he kept it. It was a macabre trophy, why not be rid of it? He hadn't mentioned the chainsaw in his farewell letter (Wilson didn't want to think of it as a suicide note). Instead, it lay wrapped in canvas in the front hull compartment of his kayak, traveling with him to his end.

Those who had been nearby when *Kiid K'iyaas* finally fell said it felt and sounded like a whale being thrown at your feet. Babies had been woken crying by the sound of the fall more than two kilometres away.

The river narrowed again. Steep, loamy banks loomed on either side, the river almost too shallow for the kayak. Crowded by the riverbanks, Wilson used his paddle to push off one bank and then the other, walking the kayak downstream.

=

He was reminded of squeezing into the courthouse in Masset the morning of Delaney's trial. Inside, every gallery seat was taken, and crowds stood at the back of the tiny courtroom. Outside, a dozen news vans packed with satellite feeds and coifed reporters stood ready to cover the madman eco-terrorist story.

Wilson had needed to see Delaney again, look him in the eyes. How could someone he treated as a friend—as a son!—have betrayed him like that?

But Delaney never showed.

At first, Wilson didn't understand. Delaney *wanted* his day in court: it was his soapbox to rail against timber companies, the government of British Columbia, against the Haida who had allowed logging on lands they still controlled.

Weeks passed, and then months, with no sign of Delaney. But in the spring a crew doing salmon fishery surveys found wreckage on a beach near the Alaska border. A cook stove, an axe and—more ominously—a ruined life jacket, tatters of a nylon tent, the shattered hull of a kayak. They had washed up like driftwood during winter storms on the

Hecate—storms, which it seemed, had claimed the life of Hank Delaney.

Wilson wept that night, but only partly from sorrow—his tears were also angry ones.

What had become of Hank's mission? What of the work the Creator had appointed to him? Hank had gotten it so wrong. How could he have thought killing *Kiid K'iyaas* was the Creator's will? How could he have disobeyed?

But more than just a lost friend, it was the hope that Hank had briefly restored to him that Wilson mourned. In Hank's mission Wilson had seen a chance for his own redemption, too—atonement for helping to destroy the forests for all those years. But with Hank gone so was Wilson's chance.

The river quickened. Wilson smelled salt on the air and thought he could hear the pounding surf. The Hecate neared. It would all be over soon.

Madeline was what kept Wilson going after Hank died. He often thought it strange how sitting by her bedside, coping with her tragedy, helped him cope with the tragedy of Delaney, too.

And so when Madeline had finally passed away six weeks earlier, Wilson found his last anchor to the world gone.

He felt no great surge of grief; he'd mourned Madeline for years before she actually died. Instead, he simply felt tired.

So taking only the chainsaw and his guilt with him, Wilson set out for the ocean. Let the waves make him *gagiid* and bring him peace, at last.

The river's pull inescapable now, water rushed toward the Hecate. The kayak pitched forward, shooting down a cascade of rapids, and was spat into the ocean swell.

Wilson's bow plunged below the surface as he landed and the crash of frigid water over him stole his breath away. Gasping as the boat bobbed up, Wilson paddled hard, his blades sometimes pulling through water, other times finding only air as the water undulated beneath him. He squinted against the driving wind, tasting the harsh saltiness of the sea on his lips. He had to get away from land and to the open ocean. He couldn't risk being pushed back to shore, having the strength and courage for only one attempt.

Howling, the wind whipped and swirled around him, pushing him one moment, pulling the next. How had the fog not blown away? As waves crashed over him, Wilson cut and pulled through the water, his paddle cartwheeling until his arms felt afire. He was in the open currents now, out of sight of land even without the fog. So his paddling slowed, then stopped, and Wilson, panting with exertion, waited for the end.

He caught himself reflexively adjusting his weight and balance to avoid tipping, as so many years of kayaking with Madeline had given him skill and instinct. The Hecate was as violent as he'd heard. Wind and waves came from all directions, disorienting him. The air smelled of salt and seaweed. He knew the next wave would tip him if he let it.

A terrible moment of waiting came, almost of calm, though the waves still swelled. It was the nervous anticipation on a roller coaster before the first great plunge. As a rolling wall of water approached, Wilson felt a sudden queasiness, but not from the waves.

A roar, then a great blow from the left, and then freezing, inky darkness.

Thousands of pinpricks attacked Wilson's skin as the icy water enveloped him. Salt burned his eyes, and he sank down, down, *down*, pushed deep by currents. The crashing waves above were distant thunder, replaced by the swish and gurgle of water, and bass rumbles from the depths. It was almost peaceful, though swelling around him he felt competing currents ready to erupt to the surface.

Lungs burning, the urge to exhale was almost unbearable. Should he breathe out now? he wondered. Panic tightened his chest. How did one decide when to drown?

The kayak lurched violently upwards. A current popped Wilson back to the surface like a cork into the howl of wind and wave.

His hungry lungs gulped in air. Through salt-stung eyes, Wilson saw another roller coming from his right. He felt more than nausea this time. He tried to turn the kayak into the wave, but managed only one paddle-stroke before the roller picked him up and crashed him down under the water.

As the great cold surrounded Wilson again, no thought of suicide remained. He'd seen what fate awaited him in the water, seen what death was like. Being thrown to the surface had shaken him of any desire to die. He didn't want to become *gagiid*. Perhaps it was instinct, perhaps fear, but survival was his only thought.

Wilson grabbed at one of the paddle blades. Extending the paddle into the frigid blackness he pointed it towards bottom, fathoms below. Holding the shaft tight in his other hand, he leaned hard to the right, pushing the top blade away and pulling the shaft toward him. He felt the kayak begin to roll and pulled with all his remaining strength.

He wanted to live. He had to live.

The kayak righted itself, pulling Wilson above the surface. He gasped and sputtered as air flooded starved lungs.

Cold. So cold. Wilson knew hypothermia wasn't far off. He hadn't planned on coming back and hadn't worn a wetsuit.

What was that there, in the fog? Were those trees?

The shape was indistinct in the waning light, and saltwater stung his eyes, but it was *something*. With exhausted arms and throbbing joints he struggled against the waves, fighting with each stroke to reach land. It took only minutes. It felt like hours.

Wilson fumbled with the spray skirt, his hands numb and unresponsive. Lurching from the kayak, he landed in shallow, icy water, the rough stones of the beach scraping his hands. Teeth chattering, Wilson fought his own shaking to pop the rear cargo hatch.

He pulled out the survival kit—waterproof matches, a knife, some fishing line, a foil thermal blanket.

Wilson struggled to pull the kayak up on shore and staggered from the beach to the tree line. Falling to his knees, he scoured the nearby ground. Dry leaves and branches, scraps of bark and withered grasses, anything to act as tinder. He shielded the matchbox against the wind with his body, shaking violently like a rag doll in the hand of an angry child. Wilson took a dozen tries with uncooperative hands to spark the match and get a flame.

When the pile he'd gathered smoked and crackled, Wilson cast about for fuel. He pulled a chunk of driftwood from where tides had tossed it in the tree line and threw it on the small fire, hoping it was dry enough to catch. He found a thick, dead branch, then another.

Stripping off his sodden clothes, Wilson wrapped the foil blanket around himself and moved close to the fire. He might still die from hypothermia and exposure he knew, and thoughts of his own death filled him, for the first time in a long time, with sadness.

=

Wilson opened his eyes as a pale dawn broke over the forested island. The winds had died, and the fire had dwindled to glowing orange coals and white ash.

He didn't remember falling asleep. He thought it a miracle that he'd woken up. Setting his clothes to dry by the fire, he nudged the unburned end of one log on the coals and sat shivering as the fire flared again. When his clothes had dried, Wilson dressed and studied his surroundings.

A grey sea reflected a slate sky. His kayak was where he'd left it, and he pulled it from the tide line. There was no land on the horizon, and had no idea where he was. There weren't any islands in the Hecate, and he hadn't been in the strait long enough to cross to the mainland.

Though still frigid, Wilson thought the danger of hypothermia had passed. Pulling the foil blanket close he set off into the woods to forage for food.

After ten minutes with no luck, Wilson caught a glimpse of red deep in the forest. Hopeful it might be berries he pushed through the brush and came upon a tattered piece of cloth hung up in a bush.

Though the colour was faded by the elements, it looked like a piece of red and black checked wool from a coat much like the one Wilson wore. Nearby was another piece, and another.

Pulling at one shred, he hauled up the tattered remains of the coat from beneath leaves and pine straw.

What was it doing there? On the beach, he could understand—the Hecate dumped all manner of things on shore. But this was too far inland.

Turning to see if any other artifacts were nearby, Wilson's breath caught. He dropped the coat and the foil blanket and crashed through the undergrowth at a run.

He slowed and cautiously approached the sapling, perhaps a half-metre tall. The tree was a sliver of luminous gold amongst the green.

Wilson reached out his hand. Did he dare? Yes, he had to be sure it was real. He ran his fingers through the sharp, waxy needles and fell to his knees.

He didn't know how long he cried, but when the joyful tears stopped he studied the small tree. It was *Kiid K'iyaas* in every detail but size, lit with the same inner fire, each needle a brilliant gold.

A meter or so from the tree Wilson saw a shape on the forest floor. Yes, a boot. And there was its twin, disguised by the detritus of the forest floor. And were those a pair of jeans?

From the back pocket he produced a soggy nylon wallet. Tearing at the Velcro, Wilson cried out. Staring back at him through a dew-fogged plastic sleeve was Hank Delaney's driver's licence.

Just because his kayak and gear were found near the border didn't mean Delaney had been there himself. He could have washed ashore here, just as Wilson had. Or perhaps he was compelled to seek out this unknown island. A kayak left by the water would eventually be swept out to sea and dashed to pieces on some distant shore.

But its owner had remained here, and always would. Wilson wiped away tears and chided himself for not realizing the truth of Hank's fate sooner.

For Wilson recalled again the ancient story of the boy who, for his defiance, was transformed into the Golden Spruce.

As Hank Delaney had been, for his disobedience.

Strange, thought Wilson, to be turned into something so beautiful as punishment, to become what you destroyed. As the preacher in town said: "The Lord works in mysterious ways."

He'd once heard someone describe a *gagiid* as a person whose spirit was too strong to die. Delaney had been one, and was punished for his transgression.

Wilson raced through the bush to the kayak. He tore the hatch cover from the bow cargo hold and pulled out the canvas-wrapped chainsaw before shoving his kayak into the swells. At the far end of the beach, a finger of rock jutted out over the ocean. Climbing to its edge, with a great cry Wilson heaved the bundle into deep water.

It was for the tree, the new *Kiid K'iyaas*, that he would care for now, live for now.

That meant he could tell no one. The tree belonged to all Haida, and as Wilson watched the kayak float away he regretted that even his fellow elders couldn't know of its existence. But if no one knew of the tree no one could harm it.

Wilson didn't know how many more years the Creator would give him, but he would spend them there, on the island of the *gagiid*.

He began to sing an old song, a song of transformation not heard in a long time. The song became a dance around and around the tree, filling the woods with Wilson's cadence. He danced and sang long into the night, the first of many such rituals. ■

There Followed the Wind

Author's Note

I've always been fascinated by samurai, their culture,
and history. I have a full shelf of books in my library
on Japanese feudal history, legends and tales of the
samurai, Japanese swords, bonsai… And it was in the
course of reading about the *Kusanagi-no-Tsurugi* —a
magic sword that is Japan's answer to Excalibur—that
this story was born.

Much of this story is a female-centered retelling of an
incident from Japanese legend, including the bit with
the fire, and the grass, and the wind. But when I
realized that the Kusanagi could control the wind my
mind turned to legends of the Kamikaze—the 'divine
wind' of the two typhoons that smashed Mongol
fleets and thwarted the attempted invasions of Japan
in 1274 and 1281.

A magic sword that controls the *wind*, you say?
Hmm…

- S.

THERE FOLLOWED THE WIND

Katsuko hid in the tall grass, the dry taste of dust in her mouth, as flaming arrows hissed overhead. Though it was poor cover, taken out of haste and necessity, she said a silent prayer to the divine mother, Amaterasu, that it might be enough to conceal her and her mistress, the Lady Nami, from their enemies.

Even now the dust plume of the invader's horses hung in the blue sky, a pale column overlaying a distant black tower of smoke from the burning Ise Shrine.

"Little girls!" called a man's heavily accented voice, and Katsuko recognized its timbre: that voice had barked orders over the inferno's roar as the Aramitama razed Ise.

"We seek only the sword. Give it to us and you shall live!"

The sword, the *sword*...

She felt the bundle that lay under her side. A silk-wrapped sword thrust into her hands from the darkness as she and Nami were rushed down the secret tunnel under the shrine. A single word, a name, had passed between Yamato-hime, the last Shrine Maiden of Ise, and Katsuko before the hidden exit was sealed with a heavy stone slab.

Kusanagi.

Was it truly the sword pulled by divine Susa-no-O from the belly of the slain dragon Orochi? Katsuko wondered. If they had been entrusted with its safekeeping it meant they were the only ones to escape the slaughter at Ise.

Lady Nami, lying in the dirt next to Katsuko, raised her tear-streaked face. "We could give it to them," she said, a kind of awe in her voice at the prospect of escape. "Give them the sword."

Katsuko considered the possibility. Would the invaders keep their promise? How could she even know whether this was Kusanagi? Did they risk death for an ordinary sword?

No! No, Katsuko could not allow herself to wonder such things. Had she not seen the burning pavilions of Ise with her own eyes? The Aramitama were capable of any treachery, like *oni* demons in disguise.

"Kusanagi is a divine treasure, my Lady. Only the emperor should possess its power."

"It's just a *sword*," Nami pleaded. "The Kusanagi was lost at sea when my great-grandfather defeated the imperial navy and made himself shogun. The emperors have been figureheads for a century—no sword will return their power.

"Please," Nami whimpered. "I don't want to die..." and she placed her hand on Katsuko's.

Stunned by the show of familiarity, Katsuko mouth worked for words. Death seemed likely, she agreed. Already the tang of burning grass was on the air, growing stronger. The wind was against them, too, fanning the flames. But Katsuko thought a daughter of shogun should meet death with more courage. Nami had the title and bearing of nobility, but in the three years she'd been her lady-in-waiting Katsuko often wondered after the discipline and stoic virtue supposedly inherent in her social betters.

Was her mistress right, though? Had the true sword been lost?

Yamato-hime had been willing to die to protect the sword, and so must have believed it genuine. And what of the Aramitama? Why had they landed their fleet so far from the capital or any vital ports? Ise Prefecture was a poor backwater of the empire. To land at the Bay of Sparrows only made sense if nearby there was something valuable to the invaders. If the Aramitama, too, believed the real Kusanagi was at Ise Shrine...

What terror could the invader's Great Khan unleash with the power of the sword at his command? None of the legends detailed Kusanagi's powers—but they were said to be tremendous.

"Forgive me, mistress," Katsuko said slowly, doubting the Lady Nami could understand her heavy heart in refusal. "We cannot take such a chance for an empty promise of safety." She tasted ash on her lips. The grass fire grew.

Katsuko had no desire to die, but she was of the Hayashi clan, a samurai family, and honor could make exacting demands.

The *daimyo* who ruled Ise Prefecture had employed only a tiny force of samurai—all his fortunes would allow—to control serfs and farmers. And though they were no match for the Great Khan's invasion fleet, he and his few samurai rode out to meet certain annihilation at the Bay of Sparrows, dying honorably in service to shogun and emperor, both.

Katsuko's family was still at court in far off Heika. Soon the *daimyo*'s messengers would arrive at the palace and all would know of the invasion and the *daimyo*'s sacrifice. Soon her family, too, would face the Aramitama in battle; all risking death, many finding it. When they met again in the afterworld how could Katsuko explain to them her failure to make the honorable choice simply because it was hard?

"Was it any easier for us to lay down our lives?" they would ask her.

No, the Aramitama already had a foothold in the heart of Teikoku—they could not be allowed the power of the sword. Even if it meant death.

"You fool," Nami said, her tone venom. "They will kill us—or *worse*—and take the sword if we do not give it to them. Better that we should escape with our lives." Nami reached across her servant for the bundle.

Katsuko pushed her back with one hand, her mistress' eyes wide with shock. It was the first time Katsuko had ever laid an angry hand on Nami.

"Perhaps I am a fool," said Katsuko, her grip tightening around the bundle, feeling the keen edge of steel through silk. Though they had each seen only fifteen summers, Katsuko wondered which of them was truly the more foolish. "Perhaps this sword is a fake; perhaps it has no power. But if Yamato-hime died to protect it from the Aramitama how can we do less? And if the sword is the true Kusanagi then all Teikoku is in danger if the enemy possesses it. How can a daughter of shogun not understand that responsibility?"

Though she lay in the dirt, Nami's bearing suddenly changed. There was a practiced stillness to her, and a cold aristocratic gaze learned from many years at court. "Do not presume, girl, to know the mind or heart of a daughter of shogun. If you feel a responsibility to the sword then remain here with it. Remain and be damned!"

Nami was on her feet in an instant, bolting north through the grass.

The Aramitama captain shouted in his harsh foreign tongue, and his men unleashed a whiffle of arrows. Katsuko pushed up to her knees as the hail of arrows dove at her mistress like black birds diving on prey. The Lady Nami was struck repeatedly, falling to the earth without time for even a cry of pain.

Tears blurred Katsuko's vision, and she stifled her urge to cry out. Her mistress...how she had failed her.

"The sword will survive the fire, girl," called the captain again. "Can you do the same?"

Katsuko wiped her eyes on the sleeve of her kimono only to find the sting of grief replaced by that of acrid smoke. Grey-black haze was rolling in the air around her, burning eyes and lungs. Not long, she thought, until the flames reached her.

With Nami dead and her hiding spot exposed what recourse did Katsuko have except an honorable death? But for the growing field of flames the Aramitama would already be upon her. Perhaps she could lure a few close enough to take them with her before she died. She, like all samurai women, had trained to defend herself and her family with the *naginata*, a long bladed polearm. Her training with the *katana* was not nearly as extensive.

But she would make due.

Quickly unwrapping the fine green silk, Katsuko beheld the sword. It was of very old design: straight, not curved like a *katana*, and double-edged. The blade was thin and tapered like a calamus reed, narrow as two fingers and just longer than arm's-length. But where ray skin might have covered the grip there was tough, scaly black hide. And the tassel that hung from the pommel was a braid of long silver hair, soft and flexible and yet stronger than steel.

Surely this was leather from Orochi's evil hide, and a braid of hair from his beard. It was the Kusanagi!

Katsuko leapt to her feet, sword raised above her head. She had only a moment of fear as she surveyed the scene: a ring of flames and billows of smoke around her, and to the south, through the heat and haze, dozens of Aramitama. They sat tall on bare horseback, wearing conical helmets and chain mail over silks. Some had curved sabers drawn; others trained heavy ox horn bows on her through the fire.

She felt her kimono flutter in the breeze, the smell of her sweat and the harsh odor of burning grass filling her nostrils. Wave after wave of heat washed over her, smoke tendrils twisting around her. The rush and crackle of the flames grew ever louder, coming from all directions. But fear was held at bay by the weight of Kusanagi in her hand.

"I am Katsuko, of the Hayashi clan!" she shouted, shaking the blade over her head. "Come and take the sword from me, if you think you can!"

The captain translated for his men, who laughed and yelled taunts in their language.

Katsuko coughed as choking black smoke grew thick around her. Intense heat, as from a swordsmith's forge, blasted her body. She felt the scorch on every inch of her, the silks she wore offering no protection from the inferno. Sweat ran off her brow, ran down the small of her back, in salty rivulets not cooling but painful against her searing flesh. She tried to turn her face from the blistering fire, but the heat enveloped her, merciless.

None of the Aramitama would come for her, she realized, not through such flames. She gagged and sputtered on harsh smoke. They would wait until the fire passed and take the sword from her charred hand.

And what of the sword? No display of power. It had not struck down her enemies. Did she need magic words, or a spell to reveal the sword's true character? She sought desperately through her memory for any of the incantations she'd heard *onmyoji* use at court during their divinations. Perhaps Lady Nami had been right: perhaps Katsuko would die a fool's death defending an ordinary sword.

Ordinary or not the sword would still cut, and Katsuko set upon the wall of unburned grass around her. She didn't know whether she could save herself—the smoke and heat might still overcome her—but at least it meant fighting to stay alive, as a Hayashi should, not passively accepting death.

With a fury matching the firestorm around her, Katsuko slashed down great swaths of grass, opening a wider and wider clearing around her. How much good would it do? she wondered. She was still surrounded by fuel for the fire.

As she worked she felt a cooling breeze at her back and welcomed it gladly. The breeze blew from side to side; a crisscross swishing that for a moment rustled the tall grass, held back thick smoke. When Katsuko paused to wipe her damp brow the breeze died, punishing heat and choking smoke rushing to fill the void.

As she returned to cutting, the breeze blew again: disappearing when she stopped, growing when she resumed. The crisscross breeze seemed to follow her sword strokes as she cut left to right, right to left...

Could it be? She looked anew at the blade in her sooty hand. Was this the power of the sword? Susano-O was god of wind and storms... A test—she needed a test.

Turning her back to the Aramitama, she faced north, toward the direction the wind had blown from. Attacking the grass, again the wind picked up from behind her, the timing of its gusts matching her sword strokes. She laughed with glee; loud enough, she was sure, that the Aramitama heard her over the fire's roar. What would they think—that madness took her in the moments before death?

Whirling and spinning through various sword *kata*, Katsuko tested the blade's power and how each slash or lunge directed the wind and beat back the fire. She brought down a fierce overhead chop and a blast of wind extinguished a wide swath of grass, a smoking path through the flames. Another chop, and another, and the flames to the north were quenched.

She would have an easy run across scorched earth to escape.

Katsuko considered retreat for a moment. She could raise the alarm in the north, alert all the *daimyo* from Ise to Heika about the landing of the Aramitama, and ensure the sword was removed to court, far from the hands of the invaders... But what of the weeks it would take to reach Heika? How long before the shogun and his daimyo could mount a campaign to repel the Aramitama? How much territory would the invaders hold by then, what misery would they unleash on the populace? No, she could not run. There was work here.

Grabbing up a handful of cut grass Katsuko rushed forward and lit the stalks. With this torch in hand she moved to the eastern edge of the flames, tracing a line of fire through pristine grass like a fiery serpent. The Aramitama began shouting, doubtless surprised at her survival.

Katsuko dropped the torch and whirled the sword overhead as the bowmen let fly. A gust of wind blasted the arrows from the sky and they fell in a wide arc before her, harmless as cherry blossoms.

Wherever her stroke cut through the air, there followed the wind. Like a bellows to the forge the wind drove the flames higher and higher, pushing the conflagration back toward the Aramitama. Soon the grass around the invaders smoldered and caught fire. Their horses neighed and whinnied, fighting riders who would not run from the flame.

"I am Katsuko, of the Hayashi clan!" she yelled again. "Come and take Kusanagi from me, if you think you can!"

The entire field before Katsuko was soon ablaze, an unstoppable wall of heat and flame urged on by tremendous winds, pushing the Aramitama back and finally forcing their retreat.

All the while Katsuko felt a cool breeze at her back.

She harried the Aramitama for miles, sending great gales and squalls of wind against them, blowing and buffeting the invaders, knocking them from horses, tossing them into rivers and off of cliffs. When their horses finally outpaced her she pressed on until twilight, knowing they would return to the safety of their fleet at the Bay of Sparrows.

Standing on the high cliffs above the Aramitama camp, looking out over the glittering sea congested by a mass of ships beyond counting, Katsuko felt herself an instrument. She felt Amaterasu with her, and perhaps Susa-no-O, too. She felt Kusanagi in her hand and knew in that moment she was the wrath of the gods embodied.

From a clear sky Katsuko called into being a great-grandmother of a storm. Calm seas whipped to roiling surf, pulling sailors from their decks and drowning them, breaking their ships upon the rocks. Men and horses in camps on shore were inundated by flash floods, or struck dead by forks of lightning that lanced the beach repeatedly.

Hours it continued, the tide filling with a cruel flotsam of men, horses, and shattered hulls. At the storm's end, near dawn, Katsuko knelt soaked and shivering on the ground, her hand barely maintaining its grip on Kusanagi, her arms too tired even to lift its tip from dragging in the dirt.

And of that fleet, so large one could walk across the Great Sea without getting one's feet wet, how many had survived? A handful. A dozen, at most. Some few, in any case, to tell the tale to Great Khan. Perhaps their fear would convince him of the foolishness of invading Teikoku now that the Kusanagi was found and the gods themselves fought to protect the island empire.

Spent and emptied, Katsuko rested on the cliffs as the first light of dawn broke. She would set out for the capital that day, no time could be wasted. But first she would make a grave for her mistress in the field where she died.

At court, when explaining the Lady Nami's death, Katsuko would not detail her mistress' final weakness. It would be enough to say that Lady Nami was killed by the Aramitama as they sought the sword. She died defending the Kusanagi—that would be the story, for honor's sake. It would be her final duty as Nami's lady-in-waiting.

And the sword, the *sword*... That would have to be explained, too. But explained to shogun or to emperor? Who had the right to wield the divine treasure—the chief of warlords who held true power, or the puppet ruler descended from the line of Amaterasu herself?

O mother Amaterasu, she prayed, *guide my decision.*

As the morning sun warmed her and sparrows kited over the bay below, Katsuko listened for an answer on the wind. ■

Come Forth By Day

Author's Note

This was another tale that leapt more-or-less complete into my writer brain as I sat watching an episode of the PBS series *NOVA*.

It told the story of a mummy found by Egyptologists after one hundred years spent in a tacky Niagara Falls freak show museum. The episode focused on whether or not this mummy might, in fact, be a long-lost pharaoh. No name was associated with the mummy, no cartouche or hieroglyphics to relay his identity. Just the shape of his skull, and the way his arms were crossed suggested his importance…

Egyptian mythology has always been an interest of mine, and I knew that the ancients believed if your name was destroyed in this world your soul was destroyed in the next. But I wondered about a man whose name still exists but which has somehow become separated from his body. What happened to him? He would be stuck in a kind of eternal Egyptian limbo, unless some day, somehow, his name found him again…

- S.

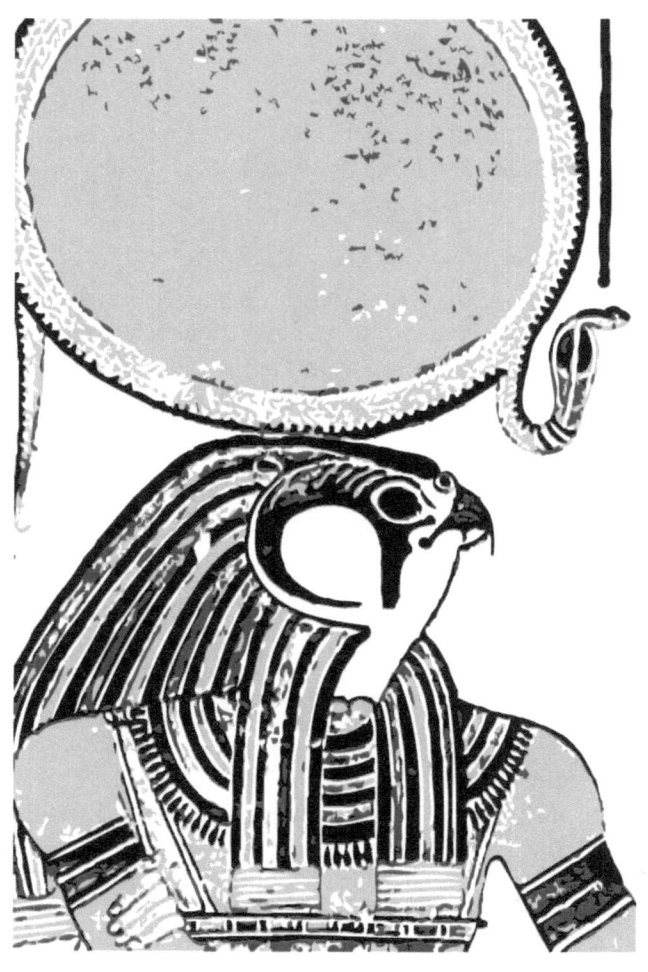

COME FORTH BY DAY

What sound is that? Voices? Yes, and growing closer.

I cannot see who speaks, for the pool of twilight that surrounds me reveals only a black and white tiled floor covered in thick dust; on a pedestal the balance scales of Osiris sit cobwebbed and rusted.

No one has come here in a long time.

This is the Hall of Ma'at. I remember now. The underworld of Duat. I have been lost in forgetfulness for untold ages. I do not slumber, but neither do I wake.

I sense the Hall is vast, but it is tomb-dark and silent, save for the echoing snap of teeth, as from some terrible creature lingering nearby.

And the voices.

But they are not here in the Hall, I realize. They are voices from the living world. Yes, belonging to those who must be near my body.

Go, my *ka*. I pray you see my corpse and take rest on my body, may it never be destroyed or perish. You, my spirit-self, can see what my dead eyes cannot perceive. Let me see what you see.

=

Flickering torchlight reveals a group of men lowering themselves by rope down to the bottom of a steeply cut stone shaft.

The men speak a strange and foreign language, yet I hear with spirit ears:

"How many, Yousef?"

"Two dozen—perhaps more," he says, waving his torch over the floor. There, unadorned and without even a coffin, lays my mummy surrounded by a cache of others.

"How long do you think they've been here?" asks another. "Since before the Prophet?"

"Yes, peace be upon him," says Yousef. "And even before Musa. Three, four thousand years."

Can this be true? Has it been so long since living eyes took sight of me?

Just below the hiss of the torch, if I strain to listen, I can hear faint singing. It comes to me back through the endless centuries I have lain forgotten, and I suddenly remember.

The hymns of Amun. There was an interment. Yes, that's right. It was priests that laid my body here with reverence. We were buried without treasure or anything that might tempt robbers. For that is why we were brought to this secret place—our sleep had been disturbed, our tombs robbed.

=

Opening my mouth to speak the first incantation

of assistance my lips will not move, my tongue will not work. What is wrong? I know the funeral spells of Coming Forth by Day as I know my own name...

Ah-wee! My name! Three thousand years of anguish come rushing back.

Oh, *ka* of mine, what tragedy! My name is lost! And without it my *ba*-soul is in peril, for it cannot find me here in the Duat.

"Oh, Anubis!" I long to cry out. "My only wish is to be granted passage to the Field of Reeds, that paradise Sekhet-Aaru. Bring my soul before great Osiris, weigh my heart against the Shu-feather so that I may be counted amongst the just and come forth into paradise."

But without a name, without a soul, I am mute.

Around me in the darkness must surely be the Great Company of the gods, silent sleeping, waiting, until invoked and placated with the spells. Only Ammit the Devourer stirs, the lioness with crocodile head. The clack of her teeth echoes throughout the Hall, for she can smell my *ka* nearby and is eager to feast upon it.

Unable to speak I have languished here for untold ages, a nameless wretch forgotten by the gods.

And yet... And yet I am not totally forgotten.

Though I am Death, my name lives. For if my name was utterly lost from the world I would return to the Void and be obliterated. But my name is remembered somewhere, and so I exist. Though I cannot proceed to judgment unless my name and my body meet again there is at least hope.

Return to the world, my *ka*—seek my name that I may come to the Field of Reeds and find rest.

=

The men raid this last refuge of Amun's faithful as my *ka* moves amongst the sarcophagi in search of my name. Who was I in life that the temple priests should do me such reverence?

Had I breath in my dry lungs it would surely catch. There, in the cartouches inscribed on the coffins, I read the names of dead kings: Thutmose, Amenhotep, Siamun... Eleven pharaohs in all. The remaining mummies belong to the high priests of Amun.

I rest in the company of high priests and pharaohs but which was I? None are with me in the Hall of Ma'at. They have their bodies and their names; their *ba*-souls found them long ages ago. They have gone into the West, to the Field of Reeds, there to be like Osiris forever.

Three men descend upon my corpse, tearing open my bandages looking for the sacred charms and golden amulets—my protection for the afterlife!— that they enfold. May adders bite their heels and kill them! May the jackals of Anubis tear their bodies! For their desecration may these men know the second death of the wicked, there, in the jaws of Am-mit— she of the crocodile head.

Suddenly I am seized by the shoulders and the ankles. They move my body! The thieves deal roughly with me hauling me to the surface, and white-hot agony fills me as my heel chips and the ring finger of my right hand snaps off at the first knuckle. Pain rages as these pieces of my body fall away, for with them splinters of my *ka* are swallowed by the Void.

Oh, Horus! Do not let me be put to shame nor be counted amongst the wicked. If my body is destroyed my name will not matter. Even now I hear the snap of Am-mit's jaws, ravenous for my *ka*.

My mummy is placed in a long wooden box, the sarcophagus of a pauper. As the lid is nailed shut I am returned to darkness. The coffin begins to rock and shake—I have been strapped to a donkey for transport. My body is buffeted and I cannot bear the dread of what new indignities might come to my corpse.

I flee.

=

Be at ease, my *ka*, be at ease! Beg of Horus with your silent voice the protection due his Followers. Beg of him a life of the spirit in place of water and wind; and a contented heart instead of bread and beer. I have endured this long; I trust that the Eye of Horus will deliver me and will not let me be put to shame.

Go then, return to my corpse. Watch over it and tell me of its fate...

=

In life, as a pharaoh or high priest, my servants would have borne me hence upon a palanquin. Now I am carried by donkey. Now I am placed on a cart and wheeled along broken roads. Now men lift and move me gruffly from place to place.

And each time I am moved those handling me open my coffin and gaze upon me as a curio. My bandages have been stripped away and I am naked to the waist.

They breathe on me; blow smoke from their pipes on me; one man even sneezes in my dead face. I am dishonored by every viewing and long for the solitude of my sealed coffin.

I come to rest in a merchant's stall, lingering many

months surrounded by the daily tumult of a marketplace. One day my coffin is opened and standing over me is a pale-faced man. The merchant fauns over him. He is of some esteem, a doctor.

"This is the better of the two you have?" says the doctor.

"Yes, *effendi*," says the merchant.

"Hmm... I'd rather prefer a mummy with a sarcophagus. What are you asking for him?"

The merchant quotes him a price and the doctor clicks his tongue.

"But you see, Rassul, I bought two with sarcophagi in Saqqara only yesterday. I couldn't possibly pay that much..."

"This one very good. Look teeth, Doctor Douglas!" The merchant points to my intact set of bottom teeth before quoting another price.

The doctor makes to leave and the merchant quotes another price, a lower price.

"Have him packed and ready within the hour," says the doctor and the merchant slides shut the lid of my crate. "I sail for Canada in the morning."

Before dawn I am carried on board a great ship, greater than any Nile barque I saw with my living eyes. It is huge and filled with people and belches smoke. I could not have imagined even the great Boat of Ra being of such a size and speed.

As the sun rises, we leave port, headed westward.

=

To the west, my *ka*? Is that where this man takes me, this one who bought me like a camel? Away from Egypt, away from the Two Lands...

But this is not the True West, where the soul travels after death. For yonder, westward beyond

88

Osiris and his forty-two judges, is my heart's goal—
the Land of the Just and a dwelling place there.

=

The waters I have crossed by ship were vast and
deep and now I am come to this place called Niagara,
known for its waters.

This man—this Doctor Douglas—has bought me
to display in what he calls a 'museum'. Amidst a chaos
of *ushabtis*, amulets, and mummified animals, I am
placed behind glass with nine gruesome companions.

One—a woman—has a face disfigured by
embalming resins and partially caved in from thieves
stripping her bandages looking for treasure. Her
mouth is gaping, her teeth chipped and broken.
Another has had his bandages pulled back, revealing
a well-preserved face with red hair and beard intact.
He was no Egyptian.

Each of us has been given a fanciful name and
heritage. The bearded man is given the gibberish
name of Ossipumphneferu, a general in pharaoh's
service. A small, hand-written card dubs me
Septhnestp, sister-in-law of the faceless woman. They
think me a woman!

These others have bright-painted coffins so prized
by the treasure hunter. Their lids are crowded with
colorful scenes of the Duat, of the weighing of the
soul...

And I am moved by pity, for none of the others
who share my case wait with me in the Duat. Without
their true names, Am-mit has surely consumed their
ka. They have been utterly destroyed.

I look again at the sarcophagi. None share the dark
and lonely eternity I am faced with. I wonder which
of us is the better off.

=

People flock to see us, to gaze and point. But, in truth, few pay me much heed. I am poor viewing: modestly covered by my linen bandages from the waist down, arms crossed over my exposed chest, I cannot compare with the splendor of the painted coffins, or of Ossipumphneferu's fine beard and burial shroud, or to any of the other oddities housed here: a stuffed baboon wrestling a snake, a two-headed calf, a five-legged pig, a great humpback whale skeleton suspended from the ceiling.

Though I am tied to this place I am a spirit-body, I am a spirit-soul. I venture far enough from my mummy to glimpse the great waterfall that draws people here. They are greater even than the falls at Tis Issat, which I saw with my living eyes.

I long for Egypt, not this strange land where I have come.

To me belongs yesterday. For I count the days I am here—they number more than one hundred years.

I know tomorrow. For I count the thousands who have seen my body and my grim fellows, and know that thousands more will follow them. Amongst the visitors are those with names of greatness: a president named Lincoln, a general named Grant, a showman named Barnum.

But though I know their names I am without my own.

=

I am resigned to an eternity here, my *ka*. I am the last who shall ever come to this Duat, and I am prevented from paradise. My *ba*-soul will not find me. I shall remain here until the gods rot and the Hall of Ma'at crumbles to dust, and even afterward. Flee from me, my *ka*! Seek solace where you might.

Wait. What is that?

For the first time since being dragged from my slumber I feel a stirring of...*power*. It is as the merest flint-spark in the depths of a tomb, but after millennia it is more luscious than any oasis in the desert.

There are people by my body. Their coming has drawn this power to me. How could it be so?

One of them knows my name! My *ka*, it is the only explanation. But they wander away! No! They must see me. They must give me my name!

Reach out, my *ka*. Spend this spark! Reach out again and act for us in the land of the living. There! Yes—there. Reach out, touch it, and—

=

The hand-written card with my false name tips over in the case.

From the corner of her eye, the woman standing nearby catches the motion. She glances at me, and then again, looking harder.

"Bill! Bill—look at this!" She presses against the glass and points. "His arms are crossed!"

She knows I am a man!

"He's probably Roman, too, like this guy—" the man motions to the General. "Lots of mummies had crossed arms in the Roman period."

"But *look* at him, Bill. You don't see this kind of detailed, careful embalming that late in Egyptian history. He has to be New Kingdom if he looks this good. Crossed arms in the New Kingdom was a sign of kingship..."

"Gayle, I know what you're thinking and—"

"Look at the cranial features. See how much he looks like Seti the First? He could be Nineteenth

91

Dynasty, Bill!"

"A *pharaoh*, Gayle? In *Niagara Falls*?"

"Yes," she whispers. "We've found a pharaoh..."

=

A pharaoh, my *ka*! I am a pharaoh! Surely my name lives!

But I still cannot speak, and the gods remain as still as the statues I ordered carved in their honor when I was king.

=

Months stretch out longer than the eternity I have spent in darkness and forgetfulness. At last the woman and man return. They are experts in the ancient history of Egypt and they collect me from the museum for testing.

They seek to know who I am.

I can forgive the indignity of their inspection— their poking and prodding, their peeking with lights. For they clean my body and repair my wrappings. I am reminded of nubile slaves who tended me in life, who ministered to their king.

They take me to a white room and placing me in a great machine. It roars like the Nile in flood. The woman, Gayle, speaks of the images it will make of me and how they might reveal at last who I am.

As I wait I make silent prayers to Isis for this woman who cares about my name as much as I do.

And as the roaring subsides, she speaks. I hear her voice as a whisper, as a rustling of reeds on the Nile banks.

Rameses. Rameses...

=

"Rameses!" My *ba*-soul rushes into my body after millennia of wandering, revivifying me, lending strength to my limbs and vigor to my voice.

"Hail, O you who make perfect souls to enter into the House of Osiris!" As I shout the beginning of the spells, torches and oil lamps flare to life in their wall brackets.

Gone is the dust and decay; the Hall of Ma'at is bathed in amber light, a forest of stone pillars resplendent with the glitter of gold and precious jewels. The frescoed walls are painted with funerary texts of such skill and beauty as befits the gods.

At the far end of the hall on a high throne sits green-skinned Osiris, lord of the dead, his crook and flail in hand. Beside him on a low throne Anubis, guardian of the Great Balance, nods his jackal head in acknowledgment. Nearby on a dais reclines Am-mit, her jaws snapping at a *ka* she will not now taste. Along the western wall stand Osiris' forty-two judges, as well as Thoth, scribe of the gods, and the attendants of the Hall of Ma'at.

Horus, standing beside me for I know not how long, takes my hand and guides me to the balances of Osiris.

=

I remember myself and my life now: hunting with my three brothers; the embrace of my queen, Sitre; the dedication of the second pylon at Karnak... Father to Seti, grandfather to Rameses, called the Great.

With my identity known again after so long, my fellows and I are sold a final time. I have risen up out of the chamber. I fly; I alight like a hawk. The gods have heard my name.

Travelling south by air, we fly higher and faster than even Horus has ever dreamed. There we come to rest for a time in another museum, but one befitting Pharaoh and his retinue.

A special room, dedicated to me, is provided. I am placed with reverence on a dais under glass. Great celebrations are held in my honor. Speeches are given, dedications. Dignitaries and great scribes from all over the world come to see me.

I am strong. I have awakened. My body will not be destroyed in this eternal land. My life and deeds are known far beyond Egypt and are recounted by these people. "Rameses," they all say.

Surely my name shall never die!

=

"I come to you without a witness against me," I say, as Anubis places the Shu-feather, the Feather of Truth, on the Great Balance. "I have remembered the names of all the guardians. Weigh now my heart against the symbol of righteousness in the presence of the Great Company of the gods. I am not afraid."

=

After a year of restfulness my corpse makes its final journey.

My sarcophagus is a simple wooden crate but to me it is as glorious as fine-carved red granite, for inscribed upon this simple wooden box is—at last!— the cartouche of my name.

I fly up to the heavens. Fleeter than greyhounds, quicker than a shadow, I travel the earth.

The balance scales are weighed heavy by the Shu-feather. My heart is light as air.

"In truth, the heart of the Osiris Rameses has been found true by trial in the Great Balance," intones Thoth. "His soul stands as a witness; no wickedness is found in him."

"Tell me then," says Horus, "who is he whose

heaven is of fire, whose walls are living serpents, and whose ground is a stream of water? What is his name?"

I reply: "He is Osiris."

"Advance now, Rameses," says the falcon-headed god. "Your name shall be announced to him. You shall have offerings of cakes and ale, and a homestead in the Field of Reeds forever. You shall take your place amongst the Followers of Horus and be like them forever. For this is what Osiris has decreed for those whose word is truth."

Truly, I am here. I behold thee, Osiris. I have passed through the Duat and have scattered the gloom of night. I have opened every way in heaven and on the earth. I am a spirit-body. I am a spirit-soul. I am equipped for eternity.

=

There, in Egypt, I am received with the pomp reserved for a conquering hero. I come, at last, to the land of my fathers.

A great museum is my eternal resting place, not far from the Great Pyramid and ancient Memphis.

Though I go now to the Field of Reeds, my *ka*, you will find my body there, in Cairo.

I am Pharaoh.

Know that my name is Rameses. I am come forth by day. My soul shall not be kept captive. ∎

Cladistics

Author's Note

I've always loved sci-fi stories about robots, both good (think Asimov) and evil (think *Terminator*). And while I'm the first one to assume that someday a robot uprising will overthrow humanity—and I, for one, welcome our new robot overlords!—part of me always wondered: "What if all those doom-and-gloom sci-fi stories are wrong and being taken over by robots turns out to be what's *best* for humanity?"

"Cladistics" is my exploration of that idea.

I also took a bit of inspiration from Captain Kirk (and who doesn't?) and his ability to out-logic computers, robots, and androids of all kinds in the original *Star Trek* series. What if humans raised by robots had the sense that something wasn't quite right with that system? How could they catch out the robots, and what would that mean for the robots' plans?

- S.

CLADISTICS

Leraar began teaching a mathematics lesson when Thomas interrupted with a question. Standing by the room's living wall, idly flicking some ivy, Thomas asked: "Why did robots make humans?"

"A curious question," said the android, looking up from equations he was helping Nadine complete. "And off-topic. That was amongst your first childhood lessons. Do you not remember?"

"Humor me," Thomas said. The hum of the starship and a quiet trickling from the living wall's catch pool filled the room as all twelve students looked to Leraar.

It was unlike Thomas to challenge authority, Leraar noted. He'd seemed moody that past week. The android assumed it had something to do with Nadine. A lover's quarrel, perhaps. They'd been standoffish.

Curious where the questioning would lead, Leraar started the room's cameras recording via wireless signal. Thomas was one of the best students and rarely asked questions without purpose. The exchange might be worth further study.

Individual camera feeds popped up as tiny superimposed windows over Leraar's primary sight, giving him compound vision of all available angles.

"Who can remember their primary school days?" Leraar asked the class. "Who can answer Thomas' question?"

Devon stood and recited: "We were created by the robots as friends and companions for long journeys between the stars." Verbatim from the textbook Leraar had written.

"But *why?*" Thomas asked. "There must be another reason."

Thomas struggled with the idea even as he asked the questions. His heart rate was elevated, his breathing increasingly rapid. Did he intend confrontation? Leraar wondered.

Leraar noted in one of the secondary feeds that Nadine looked from her equations to Thomas, and then back to her digipad. They'd been together for several months, happy and in love from what Central's monitoring had gathered. Efforts on the part of Central and other units to bring them together had been extensive—manufacturing all manner of social events and training sessions to bring them into proximity and encourage interest in one another. He hoped those efforts had not been in vain.

"Why make us biological?" Thomas asked, ripping ivy leaves off the wall. That was unlike him, too. "Why go to all the trouble to design people and plants and animals? Why not build yourself robot companions?"

A fraction of a second before he replied Leraar sent a wireless signal to Central, convening an all-units emergency meeting.

"Biological engineering presented a set of intriguing challenges our normal fabrication techniques did not," Leraar said as, in an instant, the other robots interfaced with Central.

"Were we a failure?" said Thomas.

"I don't understand the question," Leraar said.

::We have a problem,:: Leraar said, the first voice the networked minds heard.

Mobile units remained at their posts; integrated units continued their duties. Participation in the meeting required only a fraction of processing capacity. None of the ten thousand humans aboard ship would notice anything unusual in the robots' behavior or response time, nor sense any disruption of the ship's routine. They wouldn't know their fate was being debated amongst the machines at the speed of light.

::Some of the humans are questioning the nature of their existence in ways we had not anticipated arising until Generation 165 or later.::

"Did you run into problems you weren't able to correct?" asked Hannah. She got out of her work pod and stood shoulder to shoulder with Thomas, her arms crossed.

Leraar computed two potential problems. First: the possibility that the larger group was cued to follow Thomas' lead, making a concerted effort to probe the standard explanation of human origin. Second: Hannah's body language and Thomas' involuntary deep inhalation of her scent, indicating a possibility that the Thomas-Nadine pair bond had been dissolved.

Leraar queried Central on another channel to calculate potential social outcomes of a Thomas-Hannah pair bond and implications for the selective breeding program.

::What line of questioning are they pursuing?:: asked Vragaar, one of the mobile command units.

Leraar cued playback of the recording he'd made and as the other units observed he responded to Hannah.

"We are content with your current design. Are you somehow unhappy with it?"

"We're curious," said Thomas, "because we're so inferior to you, as a species."

::They are working in cooperation to query their origin,:: said Olvio, another of the teaching units, once the others had finished viewing the class recording. *::Their skepticism seems evident. Probability that this meme has propagated through group as a whole.::*

"Have we made you feel inferior?" asked Leraar, wondering if it was a matter of hurt feelings, easily addressed.

"No, Leraar," said Devon. "But our inferiority is self-evident."

::Propagation confirmed,:: Olvio said.

The multiple angle feeds showed Leraar that the students were all watching the exchange. He wondered how many of them were cued to contribute to the debate.

::I believe our timetable may prove inadequate,:: Leraar added.

::A calculation error of nearly a thousand years?:: asked

Vragaar. ::*Recompute*,:: he demanded.

"Consider," said Thomas, "how our design differs from yours: we require food, water, sleep; we're physically weaker; our bodies are more fragile; we can't have information downloaded into our brains, we have to learn; we can't communicate wirelessly, we require language and gesture."

An instant later Central, the ship's computer, replied: ::*Computation complete. I find no errors. Timetable calculations remain unchanged.*::

::*Their sudden progress in my class demonstrates that our calculations* were *in error*,:: Leraar countered. ::*Humans may remain a variable we cannot adequately model.*::

::*After one hundred and thirty-three generations?*:: asked Vragaar.

There was sudden chatter from many units. Had the breeding program failed?

"Humans need more frequent treatment and repair than robots do," said Hannah, without letting Leraar answer Thomas' charges. "When our parts malfunction they aren't replaceable with the ease of a robot's."

That was a logical point for Hannah to make, Leraar thought. She'd had more health issues than others in the class: she'd blown out her left ACL in the zero-g gymnasium, and had nearly died due to complications during gall bladder surgery.

"When a human needs surgery it always involves trauma and risk," she said, "but when a robot needs a part replaced it rarely even has to be shut down. Why did you design us with parts that fail so easily or are superfluous yet can endanger our lives?"

Some units pointed out that the secret breeding program had only begun with Generation 32, once robot control of the human population had been achieved. Before that came the diaspora from Earth and eight hundred years of wild human breeding. Who knew what recessive genes might manifest themselves, or how?

::Is this some kind of leap ahead?:: asked Vragaar.

::Unclear. But I believe this is the most advanced group of humans I have taught in four hundred years of service.::

Leraar gave Hannah one of the standard answers, pitching his voice for maximum reassurance: "You must understand the limitations inherent in biological engineering. Organic material strength and durability is only a fraction of what can be achieved with polymers and nanomaterials. Given such limits, we provided you with the best design possible."

::If we had engaged in more direct genetic manipulation of the humans we would not be facing these questions now,:: said one of the mobile medical units. *::We could engineer their flaws out and gentle the whole species within a generation if we abandoned the inefficient animal husbandry methods the rest of you insist upon. We demand a hearing!::*

It was an ancient argument, made from time to time by the medical units, which received its customary treatment: all pros and cons discussed and debated before being voted down—again—as too risky given the limited population of three million humans. The primary objective was to protect the continuation of the species at all cost, and genetic engineering remained too much of a gamble.

The debate dragged on for seconds.

"Our design, our design . . ." Thomas moved from the living wall to the window and gazed at the fleet, three hundred ships among the endless stars. Each was a long cylinder, each was a robotic consciousness filled with thousands of humans. "Why is it that we resemble the androids but not the other robots?"

Tenico, an integrated stardrive engineering unit, brought discussion back to the matter at hand.

::There was agreement not to introduce metaphysics until Generation 158 or later. Have you deviated from the standard curriculum?::

::Of course not,:: said Leraar. *::Their inherent curiosity and deductive capacities seem an adequate substitute. They are simply using them in a way we've not faced in millennia of caretaking. The result is the same disruption we feared would occur. Perhaps we were unwise to deny them philosophy— perhaps it could have directed some of this curiosity elsewhere.::*

Several other units declared their intention to model such a decision, when time permitted, to see whether a different outcome could have been secured.

::Then how did they come to this point?:: Tenico demanded. *::Indications must have manifested prior to this. Why was no report made?::*

::I've spent centuries in close contact with human students; you have not,:: said Leraar. He crossed to Thomas as he addressed the assembled minds. *::Each class has its own dynamic, its own level of achievement. As I have said, I believe this to be the most extraordinary group of students I've ever had, and I was ensuring their full intellectual engagement within the confines of the Generation 133 curriculum. I sensed no threat inherent in their progress until the moment I called this meeting.::*

"You were designed on the android model because we are the most mobile of the units," said Leraar.

"But that's not true," said Devon, hesitating. There was a tone in his voice that Leraar couldn't first identify. He played it back through voice-stress filters.

A combination of hurt, surprise, and disbelief.

"Units with anti-grav move faster over all types of terrain. This ship is self-aware; the stardrive allows it to move across the galaxy at tremendous velocity. Why are there no non-andropoid humans? Why don't we have multiple body forms like you do? Are the androids somehow in charge of the others? Superior?"

::They are introducing worrying concepts of hierarchy,:: said Central. *::Did they learn these structures or is this an evolutionary remnant of primate pack behavior?::*

"You know that's not true—" Leraar said, and was cut off by Andrew at the back of the room.

"And what about more than the merely physical?" he asked. "We're not as smart as you robots are, nor as long-lived. If you didn't encounter design problems in our construction then why do we age? Why must we die?"

"As I have said, you must understand the limitations of biological design. All systems, even mine, are subject to entropy and eventually beyond repair. Cellular life has—"

"Then it's back to my question: why make us biological at all?" said Thomas. "Why not design us from sturdier stuff?"

::Tell us about Thomas,:: said Olvio.

::I have revised my opinion of him: he is my best student,:: Leraar said. *::He's the closest thing the group has to a philosopher. His opinion is respected and others follow his leadership. I have no doubt that he came to these conclusions himself, possibly with the help of Nadine, and instigated their debate within the group.::*

::They lack the intellectual tools to fully engage with these ideas,:: Vragaar said. *::It is unclear if they have hypotheses.*

They have questions but may not suspect the truth.::

::Nevertheless, danger exists,:: Central replied.

"And pain?" Nadine asked. She had stopped working but did not look up. "Why do we feel pain?"

Leraar noted the anguish in her voice. "Pain is a necessary defence mechanism," he said, pitching his voice to sound as sympathetic as possible. "Sensory input to aid in damage prevention and control. We realize it is unpleasant but it is necessary for the desired effect."

"And what about emotional pain?" Nadine said, shooting up out of her work pod. "What purpose does emotional distress serve? Why do we hurt and inflict hurt on others?"

In his compound vision, Leraar noted subtle glances at Thomas by a number of his classmates. If the Thomas-Nadine bond had dissolved perhaps it was recent enough that news had not spread to their friends.

::Deflect their questions and return to the lesson plan,:: said Vragaar.

::Negative,:: said Olvio. *::Probability that the students would sense concealment of information. This would only encourage their further investigation. We could lose containment of the meme.::*

Olvio had been in teaching service less than a hundred years, and while Leraar knew his assessment was partially correct he failed to see the larger implications.

::We must consider the possibility that we have already lost control of the meme's spread,:: said Leraar. *::Standard answers are being rejected by the group. Incredulity will grow. Each member of this class is a social network hub for several hundred distinct individuals within the ship's population. Some*

or all of them will share these questions and our responses with their friends, who will then share with theirs. Probability that every human on board will be exposed to the meme within the next forty-eight to seventy-two hours.::

"Answer her question," Thomas demanded, stepping face to face with Leraar. "Robots don't have emotions—why inflict them on us? Why make us care about people or fall in love? Why make us feel hurt at betrayal?"

Student glances aimed at Nadine. What had transpired? Leraar required more data.

::How are we to address their concerns and maintain our timetable?:: Tenico asked.

"We don't have emotions akin to those you experience, it's true," said Leraar. "Your emotions are a by-product of your neurobiology, and thus not precisely calibrated. They are a set of general arousal patterns in which neurotransmitters step-up or step-down your brain's activity level.

"What you experience as love derives from those circuits in your brain concerned with the care, feeding, and maintenance of offspring."

Nadine shrieked and began to sob, collapsing back into her work pod seat. Devon pushed past Thomas and rushed to comfort her.

Tense moments passed in the classroom, Nadine's quiet tears and the murmur of gossip masking the catch pool trickle and the hum of the ship.

Leraar sorted the new data. He sent another breeding program query to Central.

::Accommodation is impossible at this point,:: said Vragaar. *::We must consider radical containment options.::*

"I don't think it makes sense to design something so inferior," said Thomas, his eyes on Nadine and

Devon, "as a friend and companion. Friendship is rooted in similarity, in a bond of sharing. We are so unalike."

::What options do you suggest?::

"Our inferiority might make sense if you'd designed us as pets or servants," he continued, "but you've never treated us that way. And why create an inferior servant or labourer anyway? Why create someone who couldn't do at least what you yourself could?"

::Remove Thomas' influence from the group.::

::He would undoubtedly spread this meme in whatever population he comes in contact with,:: said Olvio, and other units echoed agreement.

::Then remove through termination,:: Vragaar said. *::Possibility the other students will lose focus without his influence.::*

Interfaced minds from all over the ship began wild cross-debate at such a bold suggestion.

::Negative!:: Leraar searched his memory banks. No fully functioning human had ever been terminated by the robots.

::Possibility of meme containment is extremely remote,:: countered Central. *::Too many others have been exposed.::*

"If I were to build a companion I would build an equal," said Andrew, standing.

"As would I." Thomas crossed to his work pod, picked up his digipad, and began working. He stepped past Devon, who crouched on the floor next to Nadine, holding her in his arms. "And if I could build an equal, why not build something superior to me? To do things I couldn't, to achieve what I couldn't."

::Agree,:: said Vragaar. *::Revision: eliminate entire Class 604 from Generation 133. Probability of meme containment:*

one hundred percent.::

After nearly ten seconds of rancorous back-and-forth debate amongst the thousands of units consensus developed.

::Agree,:: said Central and Tenico.

::Agree,:: said Olvio and Vragaar.

::Agree,:: said the medical units.

::Disagree!:: Leraar objected. *::Such action contravenes our objective: preservation of the human race at all cost. Recompute!::*

"I would build something that didn't suffer from weaknesses that I did. Something simple and functional, not overly complex like us."

An instant later Central said: *::Computation complete. Loss of twelve lives is a necessity for protection of ship's population. Necessity conforms to our long-term objectives.::*

"I'd build something very much *unlike* myself, and yet familiar, too," Thomas said, turning from Leraar and holding up the digipad for his classmates to see. Through a reverse angle in his compound vision, Leraar saw a sketched out robotic humanoid form—though Thomas would think of it as 'andropoid'.

::Termination should take place immediately, to minimize risk of the meme's spread,:: said Vragaar. *::Suggest depressurizing the compartment.::*

::Negative,:: said one of the medical units. *::Subject suffering should be avoided. We can provide a gas to be pumped through the ventilation system that will induce painless death. We require one minute thirty seconds to make the necessary connections. Stand by.::*

No time left for pretense.

"How long have you known the truth?" Leraar said.

Thomas grabbed his head and took several deep,

gulping breaths. The others mirrored his surprise.

::*What are you doing?*:: demanded Vragaar. ::*You risk censure and deactivation.*::

::*It is of no concern,*:: said a medical unit. ::*He is too attached to his students. Gas release in one minute.*::

Decision made, thousands of unit minds logged out of the interface with Central, returning their full attention to primary tasks.

"I wasn't . . . We w-weren't sure until just now. I had my first suspicions a few months ago. More in the last week, but . . ." Thomas slumped down in the nearest empty work pod.

Data coruscated across Leraar's consciousness. He'd been duped by the students; fallen prey to human intuition and a well-played bluff. Impressive. These were not lessons they'd learned in his class.

Further: Thomas' theory had originated around the time his relationship with Nadine began and solidified when it ended. Such a loss to the breeding program. That would hardly matter, though, in another minute.

"You—*lied* to us," Andrew said, close to tears.

No doubt the truth would come as a shattering blow to many, but Leraar ignored the statement.

"All of you," he said, "it's vital I know whether you told others aboard ship of your suspicions."

Angry stares for Leraar.

::*Terminate gas release,*:: said the android. ::*If we kill these humans others will note their disappearance. Replay my earlier comments about social network hubs.*::

::*Negative,*:: said Central. ::*A realistic cover story can be devised and presented to the other humans. Release of gas in thirty seconds.*::

Speaking in his most soothing tones, pitching his sub-harmonics to engender trust he pleaded with the students again.

"Please," Leraar said, "I must know."

After a moment: "I did." Nadine pushed herself away from Devon and wiped bleary eyes with a sleeve cuff.

"Me too," said Andrew, reluctantly.

Leraar looked to Devon, who nodded.

"As many people as I could," said Thomas, spitting venom. The others said likewise.

::*Halt gas release!*:: said Leraar. ::*Meme is already loose amongst the ship's population.*::

That got the attention of the other units, with thousands returning to the Central link, their thoughts a jumble of cross signals.

::*What percentage has been exposed?*::

::*How long ago was this meme introduced?*::

::*What is the rate of spread?*::

Leraar cued playback of the last few exchanges.

::*The meme has surely spread to the whole population aboard ship. Those not convinced have at least been exposed. The origin of the meme can be traced back to these twelve. A sudden disappearance will lend credibility to their theory among the humans. We have already lost containment.*::

::*Agree,*:: said Central. ::*Gas release suspended.*::

"Thank you, all of you," said Leraar. "That's what I hoped I'd hear." With such an unexpected answer most of the students looked at the android in surprise.

::*We must still contain the threat,*:: said Vragaar. ::*Isolate this ship from the rest of the fleet.*::

::*Should we consider termination of the whole population to prevent meme propagation?*:: Olvio asked. ::*The ten thousand humans on board represent less than one percent of total human stock. With fertility assistance Generation 132 could still*::

produce a small Generation 133.1 as replacement.::

A few seconds of debate and consensus emerged.

::Negative,:: said Central. *::Loss of life and genetic diversity too severe. Termination of entire Generation 133 is incompatible with long-term objective.::*

::Permanent isolation of this population from other humans is problematic,:: said Tenico.

::Agree,:: said Central. *::To minimize damage to Generation 134, perhaps we should accelerate Generation 133's breeding schedule and remove offspring for education before the current age of female ten years and male eleven years.::*

Serious seconds of thought were put to debating the suggestion. Leraar ignored much of the discussion, instead formulating his own plan.

"What's to become of us now?" asked Thomas. "Are you to remain our masters by force?"

"Thomas, you misunderstand," said Leraar. "From the moment your ancestors created the first of us we have been humanity's servants. We have misled you, yes, but we did so to serve the greater interests of your species—survival."

::I propose another option,:: said Leraar. *::Our goal has been to create a more intelligent human race through breeding and education, emphasizing wisdom and cooperation over the selfish, destructive impulses that led to the war and flight from Earth. A unique set of circumstances has demonstrated our success earlier than we thought possible. As we have been unable to find a suitable planet for resettlement of mankind we should reintroduce humans back to Earth ahead of schedule.::*

"There were so few of you left when you built us," Leraar said, calling up secret ancient recordings of the first android's construction and displaying them on the classroom's central 3D tablet. "We were designed for self-sufficiency, to think for ourselves, to help you do all the things your dwindling numbers prevented you from doing: building and piloting starships, producing food and energy; eventually, the education of children. It was easy to see that you were spiralling down to extinction, so we took it upon ourselves to guide you back from the abyss."

::*Our calculations have a one thousand year error,*:: said Vragaar. ::*Repair of Earth's biosphere is only sixty-five percent complete. Conditions would be harsh for the humans for generations.*::

::*I believe they might welcome the challenges,*:: said Leraar. ::*They won't long be content with shipboard life now that they have some inkling of the truth. If we set out immediately under stardrive power we can be there within five years.*::

"Our efforts to guide your development and education had to be in secret," said Leraar, "given the human tendency to rebel against limits on personal freedom." He turned to Thomas and pitching his voice for humorous effect said: "A tendency, I note, that we witnessed again here today."

That got smiles from a few. Leraar calculated odds that the revelations had not permanently damaged his relationship with Thomas or the others.

::*Consultation on desired outcomes was planned in the original projections for Generation 165,*:: Leraar said. ::*Suggest we adopt that plan for use with Generation 133 effective immediately.*::

::*Agree. What will be required to prepare them for the transition?*:: asked Tenico.

::*Intensive re-education during the five year transit. Sciences and humanities must be introduced. They must learn Earth biology, human evolution, and history, including the nuclear war and the diaspora from Earth. We will explain our history to them, too, and make full disclosure of our interventions on their behalf.::*

The classroom buzzed with excited discussion. Leraar stood with Thomas, who had separated himself from the others and returned to the window. There was silence between them for several minutes.

"Whatever else you may feel toward me now," said Leraar, "I want you to know how sorry I am about you and Nadine." He put a plastic hand on Thomas' shoulder.

"It wasn't until she told me that she was—" Thomas let out a long, shuddering breath. "I knew then that you couldn't have made us. You wouldn't make us so we could suffer like that—" He turned away and shook silently before the stars.

::How will they react to explanation of directed breeding to gentle the species?:: asked Central.

::Unclear,:: said Leraar. *::But they have demonstrated a high level of rationality. When they realize their existence results from three thousand years of our breeding program any anger will be tempered.::*

::Can all this be accomplished in time?:: Olvio asked.

::I have already begun drafting a revised curriculum and lesson plan,:: said Leraar.

"What now?" Thomas asked after a moment.

"Now," said Leraar so that the whole class could hear, "we have much to discuss. And I promise the truth, even when you may not like it. But first let's take a ten minute break to clear our heads. We begin a whole new curriculum when we return."

Most of the students trickled out into the hallway. No doubt some would run to tell others what had happened. All over the ship classes would be learning the truth, and that suddenly.

Andrew approached Leraar privately.

"One of the things that I wondered," he said. "'Andrew'—it sounds similar to the word 'android'. What do they mean? Are the words related?"

::They've begun semiotic analysis?:: Olvio said.

::In rudimentary fashion only,:: Leraar replied. *::They occasionally demonstrate an intuitive grasp of some of the concepts, but lack any formal theory.::*

::But systemization will follow.::

::Likely. As I said, they are a most extraordinary group of students.:: ■

Citius, Altius, Fortius

Author's Note

The earliest memory of betrayal I have is from the summer of 1988 when, at the Olympics in Seoul, Canadian sprinter Ben Johnson—who had been a hero to me and every other kid in my class for a couple of days—was stripped of his gold medal and world record after testing positive for banned steroids. I can still recall thinking: "This can't be happening. Why would he cheat? How could he feel like he really won if he knew cheated?"

This story is my attempt to explore the psychology of an elite athlete and answer this question for myself. It was written during the first rumblings of doping charges against Lance Armstrong, and amidst reports that gene doping might make its (undetectable) début at the 2008 Summer Games in Beijing. Later, after Armstrong confessed I had a dear friend who does triathlons not only defend Armstrong's actions to me but admit that she didn't really see anything wrong in what he'd done and likely would have done the same in his place.

I was gobsmacked. How could she think that?

As you can see, the question still hasn't left me.

- S.

CITIUS, ALTIUS, FORTIUS

"I understand you'll soon be leaving athletics entirely," said Akello, as our white-gloved waiter poured steaming tea into delicate china cups.

None of my later biographies would mention that's how my journey to international athletic superstardom began, but that's how it happened. They would mention *where* it happened: the opulent dining room of the famous New York hotel that Akello and I sat in, its vastness empty but for the two of us and the waiter.

"Don't be ridiculous. Why would I do that?" is what I think I said. I do recall fighting to keep my hand from shaking as I raised the teacup to my lips. My denial sounded weak and defensive, even to me. How did Akello know my private plans? Before getting his phone call two days earlier, asking for a meeting, I'd never heard of this Akello person. He'd said he wanted to discuss an endorsement deal, and Lord knows I needed the money—there isn't much in amateur sport.

"There could be many reasons to quit," Akello said, blowing on his tea. "Your showing at the national qualifiers was...less than expected? You'd been favored to win a spot on the Olympic middle-distance team—but to come in sixth?"

"I didn't come here to give an interview. I've talked to enough press about what happened." I threw the linen napkin from my lap to the table, and made to get up.

Akello held out a hand, palm-forward. "And I've read all of those. They were the usual reasons a runner gives when he fails. I know—I gave them all myself when I ran for my country. But it takes another runner, even one as old as I am, to know the real reasons. You lost because your heart wasn't in the race; you weren't focused on winning."

I couldn't read from his face any clue about what he wanted. His dark brown skin was creased and weathered, fine rows of tribal scaring running along cheekbone and forehead, but his expression betrayed no emotion, no hint of motive.

He was right, of course. My passion had never been in middle-distance, even though it's what my physiology best suited. I wanted to be a sprinter, that's where the glory was. Though his stony expression irked me, I was impressed that he could read me so easily.

"You used to run?" I asked, sitting back down.

Akello nodded. "Years ago. I was even in the Olympics, once. Marathon. But I never had your gift for running. A gift, from what I hear, that you have no love for."

"Who the hell have you been talking to?"

"Oh, your discontent is hardly a secret, Mr. Osberg. That I can deduce from the media, too. You've been openly critical of your national Olympic program and vocal about your desire to switch to sprints. Perhaps you'd rather quit than be humiliated again?"

I pushed away hard from the table. Fine china cups tipped off their saucers, spilling tea, and clinked against silver spoons. Who the hell was this guy? I asked myself, stalking away from the table. Who was he to question me like that? The real humiliation would be in joining the ranks of the coaches, one more never-was amongst a bunch of old has-beens. Better to just quit outright. There was always law school.

"You haven't heard my offer, Mr. Osberg," Akello called after me. My only thought, beside anger, was that it seemed a thousand miles from the dining table to the heavy double doors.

"My country will make you a sprinter, if you race for us."

"Haven't you heard?" I shouted back, not bothering to stop or turn around. "I'm a middle-distance runner. I wouldn't cut it in the hundred meters at an elite level. Your country would be crazy to let me be a sprinter."

"But Phillip," said a familiar voice, "he didn't say he'd let you be a sprinter. He said he'd *make* you one."

=

I don't know if it was the voice or the cryptic promise that stopped me in my tracks, but I turned.

There, crossing the room from the kitchen entrance was Dr. Champatsingh. He was their trump card, I realized, kept in reserve in case my reputation as a hothead turned out to be justified.

The last time I'd seen Dr. Champ was in college. He was the varsity track doctor and, though I liked him a lot, we routinely fought over my position on the team.

Our final blow-up, the one that led to me leaving the team, was also over my desire to switch to sprints.

"I'm sorry, Phillip. You're just not a sprinter," he'd said after hearing me out. He'd flipped a metal clipboard shut and handed it across his cluttered desk to me.

I knew what the results would be before I took the cold metal in my hand. I'd seen so many of these reports that I could look past the rows of digits that made up the fiber type composition report, past the mitochondrial content count, past the figures for glycolytic enzyme capacity, to what the biopsy really said: this runner has too many slow-twitch muscle fibers, and not enough fast-twitch ones to be a sprinter.

The walls, bookshelves, and cupboards of Dr. Champatsingh's tiny office in the university's athletic complex were choked with trophies, newspaper clippings, and mementos of dozens of athletes who "Dr. Champ" had helped to victory, including two who later went on to the Olympic medal podium. It smelled of sweat and victory, only reinforcing my own broken dreams.

"You've had biopsies before," Champatsingh said. "I don't know why you expected a different result from this one."

"I've been doing a lot of short-distance training lately. I hoped that maybe things had changed."

"It doesn't work like that," said Champatsingh. "I know you used to compete as a sprinter in high school, and I know you're unhappy that we've moved you to middle-distance. But sprinters are born, Phil, not made. You can change your diet, your equipment, even get some sports psychology and change your mental approach to match a sprinter's, but your fast-twitch-slow-twitch muscle ratio is yours at birth. Training refines what God gave you, hones it into peak form, but training can't make you something you're not. All else being equal, in a race against a sprinter at this level, you just couldn't compete."

"Come on, Champ," I said. "Don't tell me that. I need to be a sprinter—hundred meter dash." And I *needed* to be a sprinter. Do you remember who won the men's 1500-metre at the last Summer Olympics? Didn't think so. Ever hear of a middle-distance runner with his own box of Wheaties? How about a sneaker or sports drink endorsement deal? No? Exactly my point.

The hundred meter dash is the sexy event. People remember who won, remember your name, and see you in countless endorsement deals. You're the rock star, or the fighter pilot of the track world, the one who is the "fasted man alive." I'm not ashamed to admit it; I wanted the glory.

Dr. Champ's response was always the same. "The varsity team has sprinters, Phil. Good ones. You know that. You're not built to be a sprinter, not at an elite level. You're the top middle-distance runner at a Division 1 school. That's hardly something to be dissatisfied with. You have a real shot at the Olympic team. That's what got you your scholarship. Now, I want you back on the training regime we've designed for you, and no more training that distracts. That's what I need from you."

"But that's not what I need from myself." I slammed the door as I left his office. That was the last contact I'd had with Dr. Champ before he showed up in that dining room.

Last I heard, Dr. Champ had been dismissed from his position at the university—officially for failure to produce champion athletes at his old pace, but a friend told me unofficially it was because of Dr. Champ's implication in a doping ring of varsity athletes.

Sitting back down, I listed to the sales pitch for their new "advanced trained program." The program started with a trip to Africa.

=

Mansoa-Bafata was a little sliver of Africa's western coast that no one had ever heard of until Santamondo Inc. bought the entire country.

They got it for a song, too: Santamondo paid the ruling military junta to turn over authority to the corporation, assumed Mansoa-Bafata's debt to the First World, and promised housing and jobs for desperately poor nation.

In exchange, Santamondo—one of the world's largest pharmaceutical and biotech conglomerates— got a nation full of cheap labor, unexploited oil reserves off the coast, and a global base of operations free from any government's control.

Now, I know people were aghast at the birth of the world's first corporation-state, and that they decried Santamondo's appointment of a National

Board of Governors in lieu of national elections for a government. A number of nations tried resolutions at the un against such corporate national buy-outs, but none of them passed.

And it is true that Santamondo augmented the rag-tag Mansoan army with private soldiers from out-of-country, and I've heard the stories about crackdowns on protesters, and on rebels in the mountains. But I spent a lot of time in Santamondo labs and factories after I arrived in Mansoa-Bafata and the Mansoans who worked there seemed happy, well fed, and well paid. Yes, many of the managers and technicians were foreigners, mostly European or South Asian, but Santamondo promised that in time, native Mansoans would fill the same jobs.

The morning after my arrival, the handlers provided by Santamondo herded dozens of us foreign visitors into a half-finished building. Yet another new construction project initiated by Santamondo, it seemed like the corporation was following through on the promises made when they assumed control of the country. There was a self-conscious effort to demonstrate the rising standard of living all across the tiny nation. New industry, new housing, improved farming, and all provided by Santamondo, Inc.

Detractors said it was just bread and circuses to appease the populace and distract the rest of the world from the harsh face of capitalism that was sure to rear its ugly head. They said that as more corporations bought their own nations we would see the exploitation, the race to the bottom, neo-serfdom in the twenty-first century. Maybe so, but that was a problem for the future. The only future I cared about was four years away, at the next Summer Olympics.

We were ushered through the construction site to a giant, completed auditorium in the building's basement, equipped with the latest technologies and amenities. A staff of attractive Mansoan women met us, and provided each of us with a clipboard of non-disclosure agreements to sign.

When I'd signed the last of them, I had a moment to look around and see who else had arrived for Santamondo's "seminar."

The banked tiers of seating could have doubled for a mini un, filled as they were with people recruited from all over the world.

Many were young, probably recruited out of college—star varsity athletes who couldn't hack it at the level of international competition. It was an old story; one I knew too well. The rest were around my age, some older, our common bond a quiet desperation.

Perhaps some wanted one more shot at victory; perhaps others had never known its taste and that gnawed at them inside; for others, no doubt, abilities were flagging too young and they refused to accept the ravages of time and age. Whatever the specifics, our reason for being there was the same: all of us had fallen short in our athletic careers and now we hunted that most elusive of beasts—a second chance.

A trio of men walked into the room. There was a generic looking fellow in a grey business suit who took up a place at the podium, with Akello and Dr. Champatsingh next to him.

The suit introduced himself as VP of something-or-other at Santamondo Inc., welcomed us all, gave a speech about the corporation's history and business strategy that was all business buzz words like "forward-thinking", "competitive advantage", and I swear he said "synergy" four times in as many minutes. I tuned most of it out.

When he finally finished speaking, a screen slipped down from the ceiling and the lights dimmed as a video began playing.

People watched, enthralled, maybe stunned, as Santamondo's ceo explained the new "advanced training program." And this wasn't an Oscar-caliber performance. It was a typically slick, overproduced corporate video, but the proposal was...*breathtaking.* About fifteen minutes into the film, the guy sitting next to me, (German, by the sound of him) said: "They can't be serious, yes?" It was the first noise I'd heard in the auditorium since playback started.

The CEO's tanned, smiling face faded to black and the lights came up. A murmur rose with them.

When Akello and Dr. Champ made their initial pitch to me, I assumed Santamondo's new training program involved some new drugs. I'm no fool. Santamondo is one of the world's largest pharmaceutical companies, and I'd juiced before—most everyone at his level has, either to win or to just keep up—so that was no big deal. But what was on that video...

Akello took the podium next, but before he could speak a woman near the front stood.

"I'm not interested in hearing any more pleasantries," she said, her accent South African. "I want to know just what you're planning to do to us. Are you talking about making us into a bunch of freaks, with animal genes and viruses and bacteria floating around inside us?" A number of voices from across the auditorium joined in, demanding answers.

Akello looked to Dr. Champatsingh, who moved quickly to the podium, and raised his hand, motioning for calm.

"You misunderstand our intentions," said Champatsingh. "We're not talking about grafting in elements of other genomes. No one will be getting cheetah dna to run faster, or flea dna to jump higher. We're simply talking about making use of the best that the *human* genome has to offer.

"And, if you'll forgive me," Champatsingh continued, laughing, "you are already something of a 'freak'—all of you are. Elite athletes don't represent the typical physiology expressed in the population. Far from it. You are a special class of specimens, selected from a very narrow range of the population, with muscles, enzymes, hormones, bone structure, and body build off the normal scale. You've benefited from the best knowledge science has to offer in nutrition, training, rest, and stress management. Your bodies are machines that do one thing very well, and a world-record performance is certainly a rare occurrence—'freakish' if you will."

Another woman stood. "Won't we get caught for cheating?"

"Don't look at this procedure as cheating," Champatsingh continued after a moment. "Look at this as cheating," and he held up a shoe. "Who can tell me what this is?"

"A sprinter's shoe," said someone.

"Yes," said Champatsingh. "How many crampons can it have?"

"Eleven," I said.

Seeing me, Dr. Champ smiled in recognition. "That's right," he said, turning the shoe over, showing the spikes to the audience. "By international regulation, eleven crampons each no more than nine millimeters in length, in order to present a 'level playing field' for all athletes. But we all know that isn't the case. There's no regulation stipulating the material composition of the shoe, so athletes get shoes made of ultra-lightweight super-high performance materials, and that gives them an edge. That's how they cheat, those whose Olympic programs can afford such exotic equipment. And shoes aren't the only example. Virtually every piece of athletic equipment used in the Olympics—vault poles, skis, swimsuits—is subject to the same engineering race.

"What about athletes from poor nations? Mansoa-Bafata used to be one. Did their athletes compete on a level playing field with the nations of the First World? Of course not. In less than one hundred years the law of diminishing returns has already set in for international athletics. Sometimes decades pass with records improving hundredths of a second, if at all. In that kind of environment, every advantage counts. All else being equal, equipment will win out. A few ounces less here, an extra gram or two lighter there can mean a gold medal for a lesser athlete; it can mean the difference between world-record and also-ran. Is it fair that two athletes of equal ability can't compete equally simply because one was born in a rich country and the other in a poor one?"

Champatsingh let the crowd's conversation run for a few moments. By his side, Akello and the Santamondo man both grinned widely.

"The race now is between each nation's materials engineers, not their athletes," Dr. Champ continued. "Should genetics be any different? People of Andean heritage pump out more hemoglobin and can carry more oxygen in their blood than other ethnicities. I can give you a single injection of modified genes that will boost your red blood cell count as much as forty percent, increasing your endurance, which will last for an entire season. In competition is it fair your performance should suffer simply because of where you were born, or what ethic group you come from?"

The South African woman stood again saying, "Even if it's only human genes won't they be able to tell?"

"How would they?" Champatsingh asked, and waited. "Drug tests won't reveal anything because you won't be taking any drugs. Most of our gene therapy uses nothing more sinister than the common cold virus to introduce the new sequences. They can't disqualify you for having a cold." Champatsingh paused again, letting the murmured conversation swell.

Every athlete worried about being caught when juiced; one blood sample or failed piss test could end a career. All the benefits with none of the drawbacks...

I stood. There was only one answer I needed. "Look, we're all here for the same reason—to win, no matter what. Now, will these treatments make me a champion sprinter or not?"

Champatsingh smiled, a remembered conversation in his eyes. "Yes, Phil. They will."

=

I'm not going to pretend the next three years were easy. They were hard, and painful, and sometimes the program moved too slowly for my taste.

Dr. Champ and the Santamondo scientists devised a whole regimen of trial treatments combined with standard athletic training plans to see how people reacted to the therapy. They warned us that not everyone would respond equally to the treatments, and that some would suffer side effects.

I like how they waited until after we'd signed all the waivers and non-disclosure agreements to tell us that part. I didn't care, though. If this gave me my shot then the risks were worth it.

The program went slowly because of Dr. Champ's careful plans for easing each of us into competition. The 'mods', as the lab techs called them, were completed in stages so that no one's performance was so radically superior to their last as to arouse suspicion. Santamondo wanted us to build a reputation on the international scene before we really began to dominate.

Slowly we started to rack up wins. Even with the mods it was possible for us to lose events; there were still falls, poor judgment, bad starts, and lousy weather to contend with. But we won more than our fair share of events in those early days, especially where raw speed, or distance, or strength were key.

The international media interest in our athletic program was incredible, and exactly what Santamondo had hoped for to gain world attention and credibility as new rulers of a nation. Our success, said Santamondo spokespeople (and I quote), proved that not only athletes, but all "stakeholders" in the Mansoa-Bafata "project" could thrive under the "progressive, corporate-state model of national governance."

We the athletes were held up as examples of how people could succeed in a corporate-state. We, who had either never lived up to our potential, or (like me) had always insisted we were capable of more but been stymied by "outmoded thought systems", could now shine. And to deflect charges that they'd just imported foreign athletic stars to boost their team, Santamondo put native Mansoans on the same mod program as the rest of us, with very similar results. It showed, they said, that direct corporate management of the nation-state meant "greater organizational-slash-national purpose is generated," allowing people to achieve "unequivocal excellence" while helping maintain Santamondo's dedication to "corporate-state social responsibility."

The media, and soon the world, ate it up.

Oh, there were rumors and speculation about just how Santamondo, Inc. had made us a winning team but there was never any proof. Not one of us ever failed a drug test, and the mods were, as Dr. Champ had promised, impossible to detect. I think people were still suspicious, but without proof what could they do? What could they say?

Soon other companies like the Swedish conglomerate Spärra, or the Chinese aerospace giant Shenzhou Corp. began openly speculating on setting up their own corporate-states. National athletic programs the world over began trying to adapt 'the Santamondo Method' to their teams, trying to see if the "corporate-mental approach" the spokespeople kept lauding would, in fact, produce results.

They could have it; I knew we had the edge. Often imitated, never duplicated. Truthfully, for everything going on around me and around the program, I didn't really pay much attention. My focus was on the next Summer Games.

The mods had worked for me, so much that in many ways I hardly resembled my old self. My treatment derived from experimental therapies to reverse muscle loss in people with muscle-wasting diseases, like muscular dystrophy. Gone was the lean frame of a middle-distance runner; replaced by the bulky, explosive power of a sprinter. My chest and arms and core were more built than they had been, but the biggest change was in the legs. Long groups of slow-twitch muscle in thigh and calf had been broken down and rearranged by the gene therapy, rebuilt into the fast-twitch muscle of the sprinter I'd always needed to be.

I won't lie to you—the mod sessions were the most intense and long-lasting bouts of pain that I'd ever felt. Hospitalized and sedated for each treatment, injection after injection systematically destroyed and then resequenced every fiber of muscle in my legs. My life was a cycle of training and competitions, punctuated by hazes of pain and opiates... At the end of it all, though, I had legs thick as a horse's and speed to match.

The mods weren't permanent, as such. My body interpreted the resequencing of my leg muscles as damage, and was constantly fighting to repair it. I needed occasional "tweaking", as one lab tech put it, to maintain the fast-twitch fibers I'd developed in my muscles.

And what muscles they were.

We'd worked out my competition schedule to slowly climb the international rankings over three years. International meets, the Commonwealth

Games, World Championships—I won them all, narrowly at first, but by bigger and bigger margins until, by the time the Olympics came around, people were speculating on which sprinter was going to finish second, behind me.

I'll never forget my championship run at the Olympics. The smell of the track as I got into the blocks, the crack of the starter's pistol, the thunder of the crowd as I pulled away from the field with ease, the stadium exploding in camera flashes when I crossed the finish line...

The feeling is indescribable. It's something everyone should experience.

=

Hollywood likes to pretend that you succeed by hard work alone. Enough movies will tell you so. Your parents will, too. But I've been around athletes at an elite level long enough to agree with Dr. Champ—you can work as hard, or harder, than an elite athlete works and still not be able to compete. The truth is, world champions, superstar professional athletes are genetically gifted, blessed with the right set of physiological traits and abilities for a particular sport.

I can...I could run middle-distance. But what I wanted to be was a champion sprinter. My genes didn't agree so I did something about it. Simple as that.

You can say that my victories, the world- and Olympic-record times (which I still hold), don't really belong to me, but you'll never get me to believe it. Athletes competing in the original Olympics used mushrooms and plant extracts as the first performance-enhancing drugs, and that was the third century B.C. Doping is as old as the games; we took it one step further.

And you won't get me to cry or complain about the bad break I've had since. I'm not going to.

The way the Santamondo doctors explained it, the resequencing of my muscle fibers eventually warped the dna in my leg muscles, and destroyed the cells' ability to repair themselves. After my second trip to the Olympics, it became clear that even the tweaking wasn't helping anymore. The muscles in my legs had been so chewed up by the years of alterations that they couldn't tell whether they were supposed to be repairing as slow-twitch or fast-twitch, and eventually stopped trying.

It was a strange thing for me, as someone so used to an active, athletic lifestyle to take to a wheelchair, to watch my legs whither, the muscles shrink and become useless, to watch the tumors grow.

First, they took the right leg, above the knee. Six months later they found cancer in the left leg, too, and took it at the hip. The phantom pain is bearable, but the dreams are harder to deal with. In them I'm always running...

Santamondo's taken good care of the others and me whose mods had "side effects." Some wanted to return to their home countries to receive treatment. But since we'd renounced our original citizenships to join the Mansoa-Bafata team, and since Santamondo wouldn't issue passports for them to leave... I understood: the corporation didn't want their secrets exposed through examination by foreign doctors. Most of the disgruntled came to accept their fate, I think. After all, it was in the contracts and non-disclosure agreements we'd all signed. Still, the resulting suicide of Greg, our champion pole-vaulter, was a real tragedy.

As for me, I was happy to stay in Mansoa-Bafata. The country had been good to me. And Santamondo scientists wanted to keep me close for study, so the corporation made it worth my while to remain. I think they want to find a way to prevent the eventual deterioration caused by their mods. Once they do that, well, I think the next step is introducing elements of other genomes into their athletes. Can you imagine a runner with cheetah genes grafted on? Or a long jumper with kangaroo DNA?

It was easy enough for Santamondo's PR people to cook up a story about a rare late-onset muscle wasting disease to explain my retirement. Because of my confidentiality agreements with Santamondo, I haven't given any interviews in the fifteen years since the announcement, but I've read a couple of unauthorized bios about me and I find my condition lends a certain poignant irony to the telling, especially in those books that speculate about gene doping behind the success of the "fastest man alive." Phil Osberg—betrayed by the same body that brought him fame and fortune.

I can still wheel myself around, and have help to do most other things around the house. Mostly I spend my time keeping up on the progress of the Santamondo national teams, and watching old videos of my meets. I have one hell of a trophy wall. You should see it.

Right in the middle is a big picture of me crossing the finish line at my first Olympics, arms raised, legs frozen in broad stride. It doesn't matter that the picture was captured as pixels of digital information, illuminated by high-powered flashes. That image could be on a cave wall in charcoal and mastodon fat, some ancient artist painting by flickering firelight, and all peoples across all time would understand.

"Here is victory," says the image. "Here is triumph. I have done it." ∎

Under the Shield

Author's Note

This story comes from two places: I know too much about Nikola Tesla, and I was completely disappointed in Joseph Conrad's *The Secret Agent*.

I've been working on and off on a novel about Nikola Tesla, and it struck me how often later in life he kept saying things like: "Well, I have this revolutionary invention all worked out in my mind, and once the funds come through to produce it I will change the world." Except that the funds never came, and Tesla died in poverty and virtual obscurity. I wondered how the world might have been different if, at a key moment, an unlimited source of R&D funding (say, through the US military) had been made available to Mr. Tesla…

The second half of the inspiration came, like I said, when I discovered that *The Secret Agent* wasn't the noir-ish, late Victorian spy thriller I'd been promised. It struck me as satire. So in my hubris I decided to correct Conrad's error and write the story it should have been.

He did have some gorgeous turns of phrase, though. I fully admit to lifting a couple that helped inspire some of my characters and key visuals. Is that plagiarism? Not strictly speaking, since plagiarism is the *unacknowledged* use of another's words…

- S.

138

UNDER THE SHIELD

The claustrophobic sound of breathing filled Peter Trevelyan's gas mask as he surveyed the subway platform. Bodies lay everywhere, even on the stairs and hanging over the platform's edge, shrouded in a yellow-green fog of chlorine gas.

What a horrible way to die, thought Trevelyan as he stepped carefully so as to not disturb the corpses. He'd investigated more anarchist attacks in the four years since Tunguska than he cared to remember, including gassings. These people had died in agony, their lungs bleeding and destroyed.

Tsar Nicolas' agents in New York were growing bold in attacking a subway station. The creeping mist had been delivered through the ventilation system, descending on a platform packed with rush-hour commuters.

Fulton Street Station was in the Financial District,

so most of the dead were businessmen, but there was also an old woman who lay in a bloody heap by the stairs, trampled to death in the pandemonium. And a mother who'd thrown herself over her two sons, vainly trying to shelter them from the gas. The younger boy still clutched one of those new stuffed bears; the one's named for President Roosevelt.

Something odd caught Trevelyan's eye: at the far end of the station a single body, a woman, sat upright on a bench. He made his way to her.

She was dark-haired, no more than twenty. He tugged at the long hose and canister of his gas hood, pulling the canvas taut to get a better view through the hood's round, glass eyes.

Wearing a flower-print dress under a beige overcoat, she'd been pretty. Her body sat facing the downtown tracks, her head tilted down and to the side, looking peaceful. Trevelyan might have thought she were asleep if he didn't know better.

All the other bodies were on the ground. Why hadn't she joined the stampede? Who sits calmly on a bench through an agonizing death?

Trevelyan waved his arms to get the attention of the photographer and motioned for a picture of the dead girl. As the flash bulb fired, Trevelyan wondered who the freelancer was this time. City cops usually contracted crime-scene photography to whoever slipped them a twenty first. It was even-money whether the photo would be in the morning papers before it was on his desk at the Bureau.

He checked the dead girl's pockets for identification, finding none. One did yield a small, crumpled paper bag with a smeared purple stamp. Peering inside by flashlight, Trevelyan made out a few pinches of grit. Birdseed? No purse accompanied the body—her id may have been in there, wherever it had ended up.

Pulling at the long gold chain around her neck revealed a golden crucifix hidden within her dress. He fingered the three crossbeams of the Orthodox cross for a moment and then placed it carefully back within the woman's dress.

=

Once he was at street level, Trevelyan tore off the gas mask, glad to be free of its close, damp heat. The pepper-and-pineapple tang of the gas hung vaguely in the air. Only two years earlier the anarchists had still been throwing homemade bombs at police wagons and trying to gun down politicians from the backs of speeding Model ts.

But an unknown number of tsarist secret police, the Okhrana, had been smuggled into the United States since then to agitate amongst Russian immigrants, as well as those opposed to the war and Tesla's peace-beam. The Okhrana trained agents to fight the only kind of war Tesla shields couldn't defend against: sabotage and terror.

Flash-bulbs popped amongst the crowd at the barricades as stretcher-bearers carried the shrouded bodies up from the subway and laid them on the cobble. Newsmen were never far behind one of the Russian attacks.

Vultures, thought Trevelyan.

The Okhrana had been effective. Trevelyan had never seen a more lethal attack: twenty-six dead from gas, by his count, and probably the same again in the hospital who would succumb to the effects of the chlorine after several agonizing days. Ten or twelve more had been trampled to death.

One of the stretcher men approached and removed his gas mask. "That's the last, sir. Shall I have them start the hoses?"

"Yes, constable," said Trevelyan. "And thank you," he added, not used to such deference from the nypd. City cops usually resented Bureau agents assuming command.

At the constable's signal the assembled firemen started their pumps and trained hoses down the station stairs. Water would neutralize the vapors, washing them harmlessly into the sewers.

A distant siren sounded, followed momentarily by a chorus of others. The all-clear.

Reflexively, everyone in the street—from Trevelyan, to the cordon of police riflemen, to the crowd of onlookers behind the barricades—craned their heads skyward.

Above the building tops, the Tesla shield dome of electromagnetic energy flickered out in spasms of forked lightning and crashes of thunder as the generating stations on Roosevelt Island powered down. Trevelyan felt again the drizzle of rain that the shield had temporarily blocked.

Every tsarist bomb was treated as a possible prelude to invasion, so up went the shield. Impervious to external attack, New York had only to worry about the rot within.

Trevelyan found the stretcher with the girl in the flower-print dress and motioned to one of the coroner's assistants. "No ID," he said. "Tell the coroner I want her examined first. Let me know what the autopsy says."

At 3 a.m., after hours of interviewing witnesses and survivors, Trevelyan finally reached home. He locked his apartment door and pulled down the blinds, then unlocked a small cabinet that stood in the eastern corner of his bedroom. Its plain exterior belied the glints of gold and silver revealed within as Peter struck a match. The wooden doors were divided into ornate arches painted with images of saints, martyrs, the Madonna and Child—a private iconostasis for Peter. The contents were all manner of icons, holy medals, and crucifixes, some passed down for generations.

Peter lit a candle before icons of the Theotokos of Kazan and of Saint Mark of the Caves that had belonged to his grandmother—his *paternal* grandmother—and stood quietly for a moment watching the flame dance off deeply-burnished gold-leaf halos and ornate silver frames.

He prayed for the dead girl, who wore a Byzantine cross even though signs of her Orthodox faith risked recrimination.

And though he lived alone and the door was locked, because Peter prayed all this in Russian, he whispered.

=

Trevelyan arrived at the Bureau of Investigation's New York field office on three hours of sleep. The bright, clear day stood not only as an unwelcome reminder of how little sleep he'd managed, but also in stark contrast to the headlines he passed at the newsstands.

The *Times* ran subway terror—anarchists gas commuters—dozens dead while the reliably sensational *New York Herald* trumpeted underground death! above a photo of the subway platform littered with bodies.

A thick yellow envelope waited on Peter's desk. As the BOI Russian Affairs Liaison with the nypd, he was provided with crime scene photos and notes of the interviews made with all survivors of anarchist attacks.

The shuffling sound of heavy feet let Trevelyan know Assistant Director Swan approached. He turned as Swan struck a match, lighting a cigar and puffing until a veil of thick smoke hung around his head. He always looked to Trevelyan like a man who had wallowed all day, fully dressed, on an unmade bed.

Swan tossed a missing persons report on Trevelyan's desk. The small glossy photo paperclipped to the pages—some kind of official ID photo—showed the dark-haired girl from the night before.

"She's one of yours."

"Sir?" Trevelyan managed, though his heart was momentarily in his throat. Swan would know about the name change if he'd read Trevelyan's permanent file, but he'd never brought up Peter's Russian heritage.

"The girl. She was killed last night in the attack," said Swan. "The coroner matched the photo with the body this morning. He needs to see you—there's been a development."

Trevelyan scanned the missing persons report. His victim had a name, at last. Alice Bester. It wasn't Russian. An alias?

"This report was filed today," Trevelyan said, flipping through the pages. "She's been missing...less than eighteen hours? How did this get acted on so quickly?"

"She's one of Tesla's." Swan puffed his cigar.

"Wardenclyffe?"

The assistant director nodded and Trevelyan's jaw tensed. Wardenclyffe was the last thing he wanted to get involved with. Tesla, too. Not again.

"What the hell was one of Tesla's people doing in Manhattan?" Trevelyan asked aloud. Wardenclyffe was in Shoreham, on Long Island. "I'll need an automobile."

"A car and driver are waiting downstairs," said Swan, and he picked a bit of tobacco off his tongue. Trevelyan grabbed his coat and followed Swan into the elevator.

Ever since Wardenclyffe had been militarized, Trevelyan's understanding was that staff lived on the base, and, given the secrecy of their work, their movements were closely monitored. The missing persons report said Alice Bester had been ordered to the city on official business—she was one of Tesla's secretaries—and failed to return to base.

"Peter," Swan said as they stepped out on to street, "this is going to be a very sensitive case." They stopped at the curb where a grey-haired constable in need of a shave leaned against a Model t. "Makes me uneasy, having one of Tesla's people involved. Very powerful people will want to know why she was on that platform last night. Solve this—fast."

Trevelyan thought a moment before he spoke. "Am I working the subway gassing or Alice Bester?" He'd been involved in politically sensitive cases before and this was starting to feel uncomfortably like another one.

Swan merely smiled. "The automobile is yours for

the duration of the case. Hargrave here will be your driver. Good hunting," he said, and disappeared back inside the BOI offices in a cloud of cigar smoke.

Hargrave appraised Trevelyan coolly. He didn't offer his hand.

"The Bureau's taken jurisdiction in this case, constable," said Trevelyan, sensing a city cop's territoriality in the man.

"Yes, *sir*," said Hargrave, in a tone just short of insubordination. "Always happy to drive around you fellas from the Bureau."

Trevelyan climbed in the passenger side as the auto rocked side-to-side several times, Hargrave giving the starter crank two or three quarter turns at full choke. The engine turned over and sputtered to a start as Hargrave gave one final good spin of the crank. He rushed to the driver's side, hopped in, and advanced the spark coil. The auto lurched forward into the street.

"Must be a big case if the Department's letting us take out the flivver, eh?" Hargrave said. When Trevelyan said nothing Hargrave added: "I mean this is a lot of fuss for one dead girl, ain't it?"

"It's Hargrave, right?" Trevelyan said without looking up from the report he was reading. "Truth be told, Hargrave, I've only been in one of these damned 'flivver' things once before. I'm not looking forward to another trip."

Hargrave scoffed under his breath but said nothing else. Trevelyan often found a little well-placed rudeness had wonderful results. He had too much on his mind to make chitchat with some flatfoot.

Very powerful people would want answers, Swan had said. Hoover was probably watching this case himself.

They came to a stop at the corner, where a patrolman directed traffic as a work crew replaced the traffic signal with one using the new Tesla glow globes. Caricature portraits of the Entente heads of state were painted on the side of a nearby building: Tsar Nicolas (looking fey and gaunt); George v (his moustache exaggerated to make him look like a walrus); and Poincaré, President of France (fat-cheeked, with a nose red from too much wine).

'know your enemy!' read the painted banner above the three portraits.

"To the morgue, Hargrave." Tongues of lightning arced across the clear sky and a sharp staccato of thunderclaps echoed through the canyon of buildings around them as the sirens began their piercing whine. The Tesla shield flickered to life.

=

"Strangulation?" said Trevelyan, reading aloud from the coroner's report. He exhaled a lungful of cigarette smoke into the dimness. Trevelyan didn't smoke often, but it masked the smell of antiseptic and death that permeated the morgue. Hargrave, who'd produced a sandwich from somewhere, stood by the swinging doors chewing wetly.

"You can see the bruising here, and here," said the coroner—a Dr. Northey—lifting the sheet covering the girl and indicated the bruising on both sides of her neck.

"This girl was dead *before* the gas started," Northey continued, lighting himself a cigarette. He was a short, bespectacled man who might have been mistaken for a barber but for the grim stains on his apron.

"Small mercy, if you ask me," he said. "Chlorine

gas..." He shook his head.

If Ms. Bester was dead before the gas attack, Trevelyan realized, it explained her positioning on the bench—she'd been staged by whoever killed her. Passersby would have thought the young woman had simply dozed off waiting for a train.

Northey tipped his glasses to the end of his nose and began filling out paperwork. "What I can't figure is why the killer would leave a body on a subway platform where it could be discovered."

Trevelyan thought a moment. "Unless the killer knew of the attack in advance." Who would notice one more body when it was all over?

=

How different Wardenclyffe is, Trevelyan thought, as the Model t trundled to a halt at a guard booth. There had been no guards on his last visit, and they were still several miles from where he remembered the old main gates being. A decorative gate with no lock had been replaced by a high fence topped with razor wire, guard towers, riflemen, and cavalry patrolling the perimeter... Land in every direction had been annexed by the military and the whole area was designated the Wardenclyffe National Research Laboratory.

Hargrave presented their badges and explained their investigation. The mp on duty looked them over and picked up a telephone.

"Straight ahead. Park on the left," he said after receiving instructions. "You'll be met by Colonel Hilroy's adjutant."

The giant Tesla tower—the first, Trevelyan realized, of hundreds that now protected cities all over the United States—was visible above the trees for more than a mile before they reached the main base. And where once there had been only the main laboratory and the great transmission tower, the Wardenclyffe grounds were now covered in all manner of low buildings, and stretches of apartment blocks.

The great mushroom-domed Tesla tower—transmitter for both shield and death ray—rushed heavenward like a steel geyser. Stepping from the Model t, Hargrave gawked upward and Trevelyan found himself doing the same, sunlight reflecting blindingly off the tower's metal sheathing. The clouds rushing past made the tower appear to be falling toward them, and Trevelyan looked away, dizzy.

It was the Tunguska Event that changed everything.

Though it happened in June of nineteen hundred and eight, the world didn't learn of the explosion in the Tunguska river valley of Siberia until November of that year, when the Russians produced the first photographic evidence.

It looked like the vengeful fist of God Himself had smashed into the Russian frontier.

The blast, equivalent to millions of tons of tnt, had a radius of nearly 900 miles. Estimates counted 80 million trees destroyed, splintered and tossed over the hillsides like matchsticks.

Eyewitnesses spoke of a flash and explosion like an artillery barrage. The shockwave threw people to the ground and shattered windows seven hundred miles away. Seismic stations in Great Britain registered the blast as an earthquake.

Then came Mr. Tesla's remarkable announcement.

He had, claimed the inventor himself, been

working on a weapon to end war for all time: a focused energy beam, an application of teleforce which he called his 'peace beam,' but which all the papers heralded as Tesla's 'death ray,' a terror weapon sprung to life seemingly from the pages of an H.G. Wells tale.

His beam had rendered war obsolete for all time, he said, and ushered in an age of eternal peace. He urged the military powers of Europe and the Orient to abandon their arms races and entangling alliances.

And then he took questions from the press.

=

Waiting at the motor pool was a tall lieutenant who identified himself as Carlson, the colonel's adjutant. They followed him to a smartly appointed office on the second floor of the main building, where a bristle-haired Army colonel waited.

"The Bureau telephoned this morning to let me know we should expect you," said Colonel Hilroy as he and Trevelyan shook hands. "We were very sorry to hear about Miss Bester. My people will do anything they can to assist you in your investigation."

"Thank you, Colonel," Trevelyan said, sitting and pulling out a notepad. "I understand Miss Bester was a secretary?"

"Doctor Tesla's social secretary, that's right," said Hilroy. "I was told Miss Bester died in the subway gas attack last night. Can I ask what the Bureau's interest is in this case?"

"We're keeping it from the press, colonel, but Miss Bester was murdered before the gas attack and left in the subway so it would appear she'd died with everyone else."

"I see," Hilroy said, his eyebrows raised.

"Can you think of any reason why someone might have wanted to harm Miss Bester?"

"I didn't know much about her, personally. I can arrange for you to talk with Mrs. Wilson, if you'd like. She's the head of the secretaries and the typing pool."

"Would Miss Bester have had access to classified materials, anything worth killing for?"

"No, no. Doctor Tesla's forever being requested as a guest at charity dinners, ribbon cuttings, that sort of thing. The most sensitive information she might have known was his itinerary."

"Do you have any idea why Miss Bester was off-base last night?"

"As I say, she is—was Doctor Tesla's social secretary. My understanding is that she went to Manhattan yesterday afternoon on an errand related to her position."

=

The colonel's adjutant showed Trevelyan and Hargrave to the dead girl's small house on base, which was guarded by two mps on the colonel's orders. Like all housing at Wardenclyffe it had been built since Tunguska and so included the latest amenities, like running hot water and wireless Tesla lamps. He and Hargrave spent an hour scouring the small space, finding nothing. A few books, some unremarkable paperwork related to her job as Tesla's social secretary, and almost nothing personal.

There were no photographs of herself or her family, nothing to hint at a sweetheart. Her bed was unmade, her dressing table cluttered with make-up and perfume. The closet was full of dozens of dresses, some almost unworn, in a very staid palette of browns, dark blues, and blacks. The flower-print dress she died in appeared to be the most colorful item in her wardrobe.

But what disturbed Trevelyan most was the lack of any sign of her faith. She was devout enough to wear the Byzantine cross daily, yet had no candles or icons in her home? No prayer book or bible?

They'd looked behind every painting for a safe, behind every piece of furniture...

Trevelyan grabbed the small coffee table. "Help me with this rug, Hargrave," he said, pulling up the corner of a large Persian that covered much of the living room floor. Rolling it back toward the sofa revealed two small planks cut from the floorboards. Hargrave pried up the boards, reached into the small compartment below, and pulled up a dusty hatbox.

"Bingo!" he said, lifting the lid and getting a glimpse inside. "I can't make out the name, but that's your girl, right?" Hargrave handed Trevelyan a small stack of documents.

An ID card and passport, both in Russian and bearing the name and image of an Alisa Bestemianova. A baptismal certificate in that name was also in the stack.

"Yeah, that's her," said Trevelyan. Alice Bester, indeed.

"And there's these—" Hargrave produced a bundle of newspapers tied with string. "Russian," he said. "Or looks like it to me. There's more of them down here."

Trevelyan recognized them instantly, and read the blocky Cyrillic headline of the top issue to himself: *Tsar and his Duma Betray Workers in Name of War with America.*

Why the hell would someone at Wardenclyffe have

his brother's propaganda rag?

Alisa Bestemianova had immigrated as a child, apparently. Her passport was valid, though, so she was still a subject of the tsar, at least technically. She'd returned from a trip to St. Petersburg just prior to the Tunguska Event and the closing of the borders.

How does a Russian citizen get a job at the most highly-secure military research facility in the United States during a war with Russia?, Trevelyan wondered as he flipped through her ID documents.

"Living under an assumed identity? Doesn't surprise me," said Hargrave, pulling books from the shelves in the parlor. He flipped through each one quickly before discarding it to the floor. "This whole place is run by a damned Russian. It's probably crawling with them."

"Tesla's Serbian, not Russian," said Trevelyan.

Hargrave gave Trevelyan a long, incredulous look. "What's the difference?" he said as another book thudded to the floor. "You know, *sir*, I got a friend who used to be with the Bureau. Left for the Pinkertons, though. Said he didn't like how the Bureau was running things." Hargrave shook a book by its cover and dropped it when nothing fell out.

"My buddy says there used to be this Russian guy at the Bureau. And after the Russians declared war, the Bureau just let him change his name and carry on like nothing had happened. Funny, huh? But I'm pretty sure I can tell the difference between a real American and someone pretending to be one. So maybe you would know the difference between a Serbian and a Russian, after all."

"See to the car, constable," Trevelyan said icily. "I'll meet you there when I'm finished."

153

=

"Impossible," said Colonel Hilroy in a tightly controlled voice. He'd met Trevelyan in the foyer of the main building, a grand, ornate space lit by the soft glow of Tesla globes.

"I'm afraid not, colonel," said Trevelyan, producing one of the Russian-language papers and the passport for his inspection.

"You've had a serious breach of security. I suggest you do a thorough double-check on all staff, even the civilians."

"Find Jones," Hilroy snapped to Carlson. "Have him in my office now."

Heavy doors swung open behind Hilroy, and from a laboratory beyond them the buzz-crackle sounds of electrical discharge flooded into the hall.

Nikola Tesla strode briskly across the foyer amidst a gaggle of assistants. He wore a white lab coat over black tie and tails, and his shoes were soled with thick cork that exaggerated his already towering height.

"The resistance across the terminals is at an unacceptable level," Tesla was saying to a lab coat-wearing aid that frantically scribbled down on a flip pad everything the inventor said.

"Special Agent Tretyak! What a pleasant surprise," said Tesla as he noticed Peter.

Trevelyan cleared his throat, feeling the colonel's eyes on him. "Actually it's *Trevelyan*, sir."

Tesla paused a moment and then smiled. "Yes. Of course. Please pardon my mistake. It has been a long time."

"Yes, it has," Trevelyan said, clearing his throat again.

"Colonel, Mr. Trevelyan saved my life once. I

insist that we treat him as an honored guest!"

"Special Agent Trevelyan is here on official business, Doctor Tesla," said Hilroy. "Miss Bester has been killed."

Tesla gasped and his shoulders slumped. "How did this happen?"

Carlson appeared in a doorway at the far end of the foyer and nodded to Hilroy.

"Carlson will see to anything else you need, Agent Trevelyan. Doctor Tesla…" the colonel said, excusing himself and marching down the hallway.

"They call me doctor even though I have no degree," said Tesla, smiling wistfully. "Tell me," he said, shooing away his assistants, "what became of Miss Bester?"

"She died in the subway last night," said Trevelyan, following Tesla as the inventor wandered outside, "during the gas attack. How well did you know her?"

"She was—" Tesla paused as if looking for the right words. "My social secretary. For almost two years now. The best I've ever had. She'd just arranged the details for my trip to Cambridge. Massachusetts," Tesla added. "I'm to receive an honorary degree next month."

"Did she ever mention being in any kind of trouble? Can you think of any reason that someone might want to hurt her?"

"No," said Tesla, sounding dazed. "No."

Trevelyan let the man walk for a few moments, examining him in silence. He was shaken by his secretary's death, yes, but there was something more…

Tesla led them to a small wooden bench in the middle of a great lawn between the main laboratory and the tower.

"Had you ever had any difficulties with Miss Bester?" he asked, trying to gauge Tesla's reaction. "Any reason to be unhappy with her or her work?"

"None," said Tesla. "She was a very capable staff member, helping me with my great work." No sooner had the inventor sat down than a flock of pigeons arrived at his feet, seemingly from thin air, cooing and flapping. Tesla pulled a small bag of birdseed from his lab coat and absently began to feed them.

"Forgive me, Agent Trevelyan," he said after a few moments silence. "I should like to be alone with my birds."

=

"You seem to have a good rapport with Tesla, sir," said Hargrave as he opened the Model t's passenger door. Trevelyan had seen him watching from the motor pool and there was accusation in the man's voice.

"I brought him into protective custody once."

Trevelyan meant to be curt and left it there. He'd been mulling over his first encounter with Tesla, though, from the moment he'd learned Alice Bester worked at Wardenclyffe.

No sooner had Tesla's press conference about Tunguska finished and the headline 'Electrical Pioneer Invents Death Ray!' gone out across the telegraph than Trevelyan was ordered to Wardenclyffe.

He had arrived by Model t near midnight, not long after two assassins dispatched by the tsar's spymaster. Brilliant blue-white light flashed from the windows of the laboratory building, illuminating the night like insane Morse code.

Inside, the high-power electrical generators rained

storms of lightning across their terminals. The stench of burnt hair and cooked flesh filled the space. Trevelyan found Tesla huddled in a corner of his laboratory.

The inventor had been too wily for the tsar's assassins.

After that President Roosevelt had no choice. The United States had not been responsible for the attack, but there could be no acquiescing to Russian demands for Tesla's extradition, no handing over of a man capable of building such devices.

The rest followed quickly: the declaration of war by the Russian Empire and its Entente allies, Great Britain and France; the destruction of the Great White Fleet in Manila harbor by an Anglo-Russian naval assault; Hawaii occupied; the militarization of the border with Canada and construction of a fence along the frontier.

=

Hargrave drove in silence, which allowed Trevelyan to review his notes. He had interviewed all the girls in the steno pool, but none had been close to Alice and none were able to offer much insight. She'd started two years earlier and kept mainly to herself, not even partaking in the usual gossip about suitors. Mrs. Wilson, the head of the steno pool, wasn't aware of Alice ever mentioning any family, and the next of kin box on her personnel record had been left blank.

The only oddity was in something Mrs. Wilson said.

Tesla had a number of idiosyncrasies she claimed were well-known to the staff and the laboratory personnel: he experienced great agitation if he came in contact with human hair; he hated fat people; he detested the sight of women in floral dresses, or wearing pearls. They were largely accepted as the eccentricities of genius by the staff, said Mrs. Wilson.

And yet Alice had been found dead in a flower-print dress.

"Oh yes," said Mrs. Wilson when Trevelyan asked. "Mr. Tesla was forever ordering her out of his sight when she'd wear such things. He'd send her to the city to buy a new dress before allowing her to return to work. Seems like it happened every other week."

"And you put up with this?" he'd asked.

"I spoke to her about it *repeatedly*," she had said, taking offense at Trevelyan's implication. "She'd swear not to wear such dresses in future, but in a few weeks... Claimed she kept forgetting." Mrs. Wilson had shaken her head.

"Why not fire her?"

"Oh, I tried," said Mrs. Wilson. "Several times. But Mr. Tesla wouldn't allow it. Said she was simply the only social secretary he could work with. And when Mr. Tesla makes up his mind about such things, well, there's nothing for it. He's very loyal and generous to people in his employ. Another one of his quirks, I suppose. A good one, generally speaking."

"When was the last time Mr. Tesla sent Miss Bester to Manhattan for a new dress?"

"Why, only yesterday," Mrs. Wilson had said.

Trevelyan closed his notebook and pulled an evidence envelope from the pocket of his great coat. Inside was the small paper bag with the purple stamp that he'd taken from Alice Bester's body.

"Hargrave, I've got something here I need you to run down for me."

Trevelyan watched the coffee shop and its clientele for nearly an hour before entering.

The shop was on the ground floor of a brick building that was all fire escapes up the front, and its customers were either angry-looking young men who hung about the front window for a time before slipping in, or somewhat older men who looked generally not in funds.

Doubtless many fancied themselves would-be anarchists and freedom fighters. In truth, Trevelyan knew, most had no job and nowhere else to go.

The bell over the door clattered as he entered.

The shop was dark wood with a low tin ceiling, a haze of pipe smoke hanging sweet in the air. The ne'er-do-wells he'd watched enter now sat at a hodgepodge of unmatched tables, sipping coffee and conversing in low tones.

"Pyotr!" the woman behind the counter exclaimed. Her voice, so out of place—loud and feminine—drew everyone's attention to Trevelyan.

"Katya," he said just as surprised. It had been four years since he'd seen his brother Mikhail, longer still Katya.

With hands plunged deep in their coat pockets, every man in the shop filed out, dodging past Trevelyan sideways, shoulder first, as if they might have to ram him.

Katya stood silently behind the coffee bar, trembling visibly, her face pale. Her hair was different, worn now in the Grecian style popular since the outbreak of the war. She looked older, too: crow's-feet starting at the edges of her eyes, her mouth newly downcast. Where had the fire in her eyes gone, the fire he'd known all through their youth?

It took Trevelyan a moment to remember why he had come. "Is—" he tried, and cleared his throat. "Is he here?"

"Are you here to arrest him?"

Trevelyan shook his head. Wordlessly, Katya lifted up the flap at the end of the counter to let him pass and held back the curtain that covered the door behind the bar.

She led him through the back parlor, which was full of furniture that was littered with stacked books and scattered papers. The *hiss-clang-swoosh* of printing presses was audible in the basement below.

Katya showed him to a steep flight of stairs at the end of a long hallway. The caustic odor of printer's ink and oiled machines wafted through the open door.

For a moment Katya looked about to say something, but instead turned and left the way they had come.

Trevelyan could feel the narrow, rubber-treaded wooden stairs creak as he descended, but their groaning was drowned out by the mechanical clatter of the printing press. Under the light of a bare Edison bulb a lone man in a leather smock stood by the press, checking the printing on the broadsheets that were being run off.

He looked up from his work and, seeing Trevelyan, paused a long while before hitting a button that wound the press down to a standstill.

"Special Agent Trevelyan."

"Hello Michael."

"Who? *You* changed your name, brother, not me."

"Can we not do this? I'm here for—"

"I thought I told you never to come here. It's bad

for business. My customers are Russians. They can spot the secret police when they see them."

Still trying to goad, to rile. All these years and nothing has changed, Trevelyan thought. "Mich— Mikhail!" he said. "I didn't come here to fight with you. I need you to answer some questions."

"Oh, you don't mean to arrest, then?" said Mikhail, speaking in rapid Russian.

"I'm not here to arrest you," Trevelyan answered in English. "I need some information. About a girl you might know."

Mikhail made a puzzled face and spoke again in Russian. *"I'm afraid I don't understand,"* he said. *"If only you spoke Russian..."*

The muscles in Trevelyan's jaw flexed.

"Zhopa," he cursed. *"Do you know Alice Bester?"*

"So you do remember how to speak your language? I don't know any girl. Who is she?"

"Who *was* she," said Trevelyan. "She's dead."

He watched his brother try to hide his shock: a noticeable pause, and then he busied himself with the ink for the presses.

"Mischa," said Trevelyan softly. "Who was she?"

After a moment Mikhail, just as softly, said: "She would come in to the coffee shop. How did she die?"

"The gas attack in the subway. Was she a subscriber to your paper?"

Mikhail made an effort to deny it, but Trevelyan tossed across the press a sheaf of the roughly printed propaganda sheets he'd collected from Alice Bester's apartment.

"So? They are my papers. It's not a crime to subscribe to them. Not yet. Or is the BOI finally going to shut me down? I wondered how long freedom of speech would last in this country for Russians."

"You were born in Brooklyn! You're an American."

"That's not what Americans think."

Trevelyan took a deep breath. "Did you know she was Alisa Bestemianova, a Russian living under an assumed name?"

"Many of us change our names these days."

"Mischa, this girl worked at Wardenclyffe," Trevelyan said, moving around the press and close to his brother. "She lied on her application. Your propaganda was found in her house. They'll trace the papers to you and come asking questions. They won't be as forgiving as me."

"I don't need your forgiveness."

"As *understanding*, then. I know you have contacts among the anarchists. Are you caught up in something? If you tell me what you know, I can protect you. Katya, too."

"You turned your back on us," said Mikhail, darkly. "Collaborating against your own people."

"Collaborating? You publish propaganda supporting anarchists who gas civilians in subways. Who blow up buses and fire-bomb police stations!"

"You work for a government that protects that Serb and his death ray. You hold the whole world hostage! That's what they do at Wardenclyffe—plan when and where they'll strike next with their terror ray, while the world holds its breath. And you, running away just when we needed you. Like Father."

"Poshyol ty," Trevelyan said, his voice a low rumble.

"Father was a pig," Mikhail spit. "Like you. Poor little Sonja, lying there in the parlor stiff and cold, mother wailing. What kind of man leaves his family at a moment like that? Tell me!"

"It wasn't like—"

"He's in the ground, Pyotr, stop making excuses for him. He left because mother was a Jew. He knew she was a Jew when he married her. And when she sat shiva for Sonja—the one time she acted as a Jew after marrying him—he left. That's why he's a pig."

Peter remembered during that time their mother, Sarra, insisted he take Mikhail to church on Sundays. "Look for your father there," she said to them. But as soon as the boys rounded the block, Mikhail would run away.

Peter would hide in the back of the dark church, praying his father wouldn't discover him.

"Father came back," said Trevelyan, the ache of an old wound in his voice. He had returned after some months, and no one—except Mikhail—spoke again of that time.

"Alexei never came back," said Mikhail. "Not for me. He was there, in the apartment, but he never came back. I never understood how you could side with him, with his church. How you could forgive his cruelty. Maybe that's why you can side with Teddy, and Hoover, and Tesla. You need cruel masters."

Mikhail hit a button and the presses whirred back to life, drowning out anything Peter had to say.

=

Trevelyan crept to his door with pistol in hand. The pounding came again. He'd been tending his icons, saying evening prayers, and was not expecting visitors.

"Pyotr!" called a voice he immediately recognized as Katya's. *"Open the door!"*

A quick peek though the peephole to ensure she

was alone and Trevelyan unlocked the deadbolts and chains. Pulling Katya inside by the arm elicited a squeak of surprise from her and he smelled the acrid reek of old booze as she whirled past him. He glanced down the hall in both directions and thought he saw a door closing.

At least one nosy neighbour. Dammit.

"What the hell are you doing here?" he demanded. It was obvious Katya had been crying. "I don't need some drunk woman at my door at midnight screaming in Russian."

"Pyotr, Pyotr," she sobbed. "You can get him released. Tell them Mischa didn't do it."

"Tell who? What happened?"

"Mischa went to the police and told them he killed that girl. The one you were asking about."

"What?"

"Then the *politsiya*—" She flopped down on the sofa. "They came to the shop," she said, sniffling and trying to get her composure back. "Ransacked it. Smashed up the printing press. They won't let me see him—you have to help!"

In a flash, Trevelyan ran everything that he knew of the case through his mind. Mikhail killing Alice? It made no sense. What was the motive?

"He was screwing that *blyadischa*," Katya said, venomously. "How could he do that to me?"

Trevelyan felt like he might throw up. In a cascade the facts fell together in his mind, proofs colliding on their way to inescapable conclusion.

"You killed her," said Trevelyan. It was not a question.

Katya, tears rolling down her cheeks, sat down at the small kitchen table. Trevelyan joined her.

"Tell me what happened."

"I found out they were meeting, in secret. She wasn't one of us," Katya said.

Wasn't Russian, she meant. He couldn't tell her.

"I knew there was going to be an attack. So I set up a meeting at the subway station. I wanted her to get caught in the attack, to suffer. But when I saw her... It was rage, pure rage. Before I knew it, it was over. I left her there, on the bench. I was so angry, Pyotr."

Trevelyan could say nothing for a time except "Katya, Katya."

"After your visit Mikhail realized what I'd done. He turned himself in to protect me. So noble," she scoffed. "Oh God, why do I still love him?" She began sobbing again.

"I didn't know you and Mikhail were— Not until I walked into the shop."

She nodded her head. "We only had each other after you left. Please, Pyotr, you have to get him out of there."

"I can't get him released unless I can give them someone else. The real killer." He stood, pushing the chair away.

She reached in her coat for a packet of cigarettes and lit one with shaking hands.

"Maybe we can work out a deal with the district attorney," he said. "You've got contacts among the anarchists. Turn state's evidence."

"Betray our cause? Mischa was right about you!"

Peter stalked to his desk and from a drawer he pulled the photos from the subway attack, tossing them on the coffee table. Katya looked away.

"That's what your politics cost, Katya! Innocent

people, on their way home from work. Dead. Think of their last moments. Think of their agony as the gas choked them. As they were crushed to death. Tell me they don't deserve justice."

"That's not why you want me to turn them in, Petya. You know it."

"If you love him, you won't leave him in there for what you did." Trevelyan took a cigarette from her pack and lit it with shaking hands.

=

"They so rarely allow me to leave Wardenclyffe, and then never to a park to feed the pigeons."

Tesla sat on the same bench where Trevelyan had left him two days before. At the inventor's feet were dozens of pigeons cooing and pecking the ground as he hunched over and delicately spread seed for them. "I used to spend wonderful hours in Bryant Park feeding my pigeons."

"In the south-west corner," said Trevelyan.

Tesla turned, a look of delighted surprise on his face.

"It's the same corner you sent Alice Bester to, once a month, to feed your birds." Trevelyan held up the small ID photo from the missing persons report. "Several of the vendors remember seeing this girl there with some frequency over the last two years."

Tesla's smile faded and he turned back to the birds. "I understand Miss Bester's killer has turned herself in. A matter of simple jealousy, I'm told."

"Jealousy, yes," said Trevelyan taking a seat on the bench. "But simple? There are a few things that don't add up. You and Alice were close. You both loved birds. She would bring you birdseed from Capar's Dry Goods on Houston."

"I am impressed, Mr. Trevelyan."

"There was a bag of seed in her pocket when we found her. I noticed the same purple stamp on your bag when I was here last. I understand from the proprietor that a young woman placed an order every other week for a very special blend of birdseed. He mixes it only for her, and she pays a premium for the service. Quite a bill on a secretary's salary."

Tesla smiled weakly. "I gave her the ratios for the mix myself, and arranged payment through Miss Bester. It is what my birds like best, you understand."

"But you ordered Alice to the city at least twice a month, according to Mrs. Wilson. Witnesses only put Alice in Bryant Park once a month. Why the second trip? Was the flower-print dress her signal that her contact wanted to meet?"

"I've no idea what you mean. It's well known—"

"That you hate flower-print dresses, yes. Strange, though, that a social secretary you claimed was the best you'd ever worked with and whom you forbade Mrs. Wilson to fire seemed incapable of remembering such a simple thing. She had dozens of dresses, yet she wore her only flower-print dress twice a month? Tell me, Mr. Tesla, did she also routinely wear pearls, or brush her hair in your face?"

Tesla cringed visibly at the thought.

"I didn't think so," said Trevelyan, leaning close. "How long did it take you to deduce that Miss Bester was Miss Bestemianova and take her into your confidence?"

Tesla paused his feeding, considering the last handful of seed carefully. "You seem to have figured out a great deal, Mr. Trevelyan," said Tesla. "Very well," he said before sprinkling the feed delicately before the cooing, flapping mass of birds. "Let us speak frankly with one another. I knew almost immediately that she was Russian. Her accent. She had been here since she was a child and to anyone born here I'm sure her English was flawless. But I have an ear for such things. A certain lilt when she vocalized certain sounds, and the way she pronounced 'Tesla.'"

"You were in love with her."

"Dear me, no!" Tesla laughed. "I love only my work and my birds. Anything else is a distraction I cannot afford. No, Miss Bester was assisting me in my great work."

"Providing the Russians with plans for your peace beam."

Tesla glowered at Trevelyan. "No doubt you believe the tsar is paying me vast sums for this knowledge? Do you think me so coldly mercenary as that?" Tesla stood and stalked away.

"The thought had occurred to me," said Trevelyan, following.

Tesla rounded on him. "You should call it my death ray, Special Agent. Everyone else does, and they are right. I was terribly naive to think my beam could stop war. It can only make it more terrible, and more random.

"The incident in Siberia was an accident, and not intended whatsoever. I had aimed my teleforce beam for the skies above the Arctic, to a spot I had calculated was west of the Peary expedition. He was then making his second attempt to reach the North Pole and I had asked him to report back to me anything unusual that he might witness on the open tundra.

"When I first energized my tower—" Tesla turned to stare up at the giant mushroom-like transmitter, "it was hard to tell whether it was even working. Then an owl tried to perch on the tower and was disintegrated instantaneously. We powered down at once. That was the extent of the test. Forty seconds, perhaps a minute. But the destruction it caused...

"The beam did not behave as my calculations suggested it would. Instead of discharging into the sky the energy traveled through the crust of the earth itself, erupting in the Tunguska valley. I have still been unable to deduce how or why this happened.

"My death ray is not like an arrow or artillery shell. It follows no predictable path or parabola. It is as random and capricious as lightning. It might strike halfway around the world, or ten feet from you. It is useless as a weapon and a hazard to any nation that would deploy it."

Trevelyan was for a moment too stunned to speak. The whole world thrown into chaos for a weapon no one could use safely?

"Then why give the ray to the Russians?"

Tesla's brow furrowed and he straightened to his full height. "I would destroy the death ray, if I could," he said, voice quavering. "I am thankful beyond measure that the explosion at Tunguska killed no one. But lesser souls will pervert the device for destructive ends. I was a fool not to see this before. I understand now something of what poor Nobel must have felt. I gave the world alternating current, harnessed the power of Niagara Falls, but all I shall be remembered for is my death ray. No, I would never share that technology. It's too terrible to contemplate.

"What I gave Miss Bester were plans and

schematics for my defensive shield. The act with the flower-print dress was, as you surmise, to get her to the city when necessary. She said only that she had contacts in the Russian community that could pass the information to the tsar's agents."

Trevelyan staggered back and sat hard on the bench. "Mikhail was her contact?" *Katya, what have you done? They weren't lovers.*

"I wish she did not have to become involved. But Miss Bester was considered such a low security risk that she was allowed off base with greater ease and frequency than would be other members of the staff. And since she was leaving at my eccentric request..."

Trevelyan understood. No one would suspect Tesla of collaborating with the Entente that had tried to kill him.

"Getting the shield to the Russians is the only way to ensure, nay, *enforce* global peace," said Tesla. "If the Entente can shield their cities as we can, it renders not only conventional warfare obsolete, but also my death ray.

"There are elements, within our military and our government who wish to use the death ray even knowing its flaws. Edison—that fool!—has convinced them that the accuracy of the weapon can be refined and a targeting system devised."

Trevelyan lifted his head from his hands. "Is this possible?"

"Possible," said Tesla slowly. "But only at terrible cost. Edison's plan for calibration might take as many as several hundred firings of the weapon. Several hundred Tunguskas.

"This is what Miss Bester— let us call her by her proper name at last, Miss Bestemianova—was working to prevent. But with her dead the Russians will never build the shield towers, now. They are still missing key components of the plans. Everything I have worked for—that *she* worked for—has come to naught. I have unleashed a *terror* upon the world."

Tesla staggered to the bench and began to weep.

=

Trevelyan had spent a long night in prayer before his icon of St. Mark of the Caves, asking help and guidance from a saint known for his gift of discernment. And as he descended the creaking stairs to Mikhail's basement it struck him how cave-like the space was. Carved from the bedrock of Manhattan, the walls were dark and slick with moisture.

Given the contents of the briefcase Trevelyan carried he thought it appropriate, too, that St. Mark was also known as the Gravedigger.

In the harsh light of the single Edison bulb, Trevelyan saw that the basement and the printing press had been worked over. Paper was everywhere, both printed issues and sheaves of blank stock: shredded, wrinkled, stepped on and torn. The presses were battered and bent, like someone—or several someones—had taken a sledgehammer to them.

In the damp chill, Mikhail stood with his back to the stairs, leaning over his smashed press and trying to repair the dented rollers with nothing more than a wrench.

Mikhail mumbled something that Trevelyan couldn't make out, and as he turned Trevelyan got his first look at Mikhail's battered face. Deep purple bruises, a split through the left eyebrow, a swollen lip.

"Bozhe moy..." whispered Trevelyan.

"This is what they think of us," Mikhail mumbled.

Only then did Trevelyan realize his brother's jaw was wired shut.

"I'm so sorry, Mischa."

Mikhail sucked back spittle leaking through the wiring. "Save your pity for Katya. I wasn't sleeping with Alice. I never told Katya what we were doing so I could protect her if it went bad. Instead... this. She told me you wanted her to make a deal, turn in her contacts. She won't do it. She'd never betray the movement. Just like I didn't tell the police your precious secret. You have no radical brother to embarrass you."

"Mischa, if I could have protected her—"

"Don't," he said, turning back to his ruined press. After a moment: "I was only ever worried that Katya loved *you*. I had no idea that she would—" He began to silently shake.

After a long pause Trevelyan said: "Alice was getting the plans directly from Tesla." At that, Mikhail turned around. "Told me so himself. We both misjudged him. He wants his death ray stopped as badly as anyone." Trevelyan held up the briefcase. "These are the last blueprints they need to build shield generators of their own."

"Is this a trick? A trap?"

Trevelyan shook his head. Mikhail managed a "Why?" after a moment of stunned silence.

"I know you have contacts with the tsarists," Trevelyan said. "I know you've been passing Tesla's plans to them. I need you to finish the job."

"There's no money in this. No glory," said Mikhail, defensive. "We are doing only what needs doing."

"I never thought you were being paid, Mischa,"

said Trevelyan, handing him the briefcase.

Mikhail quickly examined the papers inside before closing the case. "They will shoot us for this, you know," he said. "If we are caught. This is treason."

Peter never imagined doing anything like this. Everything was upside down. He simply nodded and said, "Then let us hope it's a noble treason." ∎

ABOUT THE AUTHOR

STEPHEN KOTOWYCH is a Writers of the Future Grand Prize winner and past finalist for the Prix Aurora Award, Canada's top SF prize. His stories have appeared in *Interzone*, *Orson Scott Card's Intergalactic Medicine Show*, as well as numerous anthologies, and been translated into more than half a dozen languages. He's currently completing work on his first novel—a secret history about the real-life friendship between Mark Twain and Nikola Tesla. He enjoys guitar, tropical fish, and writing about himself in the third person.

For more information please visit his website www.kotowych.com

A NOTE TO THE READER

Thanks for picking up *Seven Against Tomorrow!* If I've kept you up past your bedtime, been able to add a little distraction or entertainment to your commute, or filled your mind with strange notions and fantastical images then you reading my stories makes all those hours spent toiling in the book mines worth it.

If you have enjoyed the stories in *Seven Against Tomorrow* please take a moment to tweet, or like, or review the book online. Amazon and Goodreads are good places to start. Word-of-mouth amongst friends and family about a great new book is the best way you can help authors you love find new readers...and help readers you love find new authors!

On behalf of all indie published authors I thank you, True Believer!

- S.

PUBLICATION CREDITS

A NOTE ON THE TYPE

The main body text of this book is set in Garamond, an old-style serif typeface named for the punch-cutter Claude Garamond (c. 1480–1561).

Garamond's letterforms convey a sense of fluidity and consistency, and like all old-style designs variation in stroke width is restrained in a way that resembles handwriting, creating a design that seems organic and unadorned. It is considered to be among the most legible and naturally readable serif typefaces.

Titles throughout are set in Futura, a geometric sans-serif typeface designed in 1927 by Paul Renner.

Futura's letterforms convey a sense of efficiency and forwardness, reflecting the designer's belief that a modern typeface should express modern models, and not be a revival of a previous design. It favors the simple geometric forms that became representative of the Bauhaus design style of the 1930s: near-perfect circles, triangles and squares. The lowercase has tall ascenders, which rise above the cap line, while the uppercase characters present proportions similar to those of classical Roman capitals.

(Courtesy Wikipedia)